Reader

Mhairi O'Reilly

"Sometimes, the broken pieces of two souls fit together perfectly—

healing scars, silencing fears, and proving that even in the darkest

of worlds, love can be the light that saves us."

1

Prologue

Pride and Prejudice was my all-time favorite romance. Elizabeth Bennet and Mr. Darcy overcame everything—pride, prejudice, and all the expectations of their world—to realize they belonged together. I fantasized that one day, my Mr. Darcy would come along. But deep down, I knew it was just that: a fantasy.

At the young age of nineteen, I had given up on fairy-tales.

With a sigh, I closed the book and let the silence settle around me. Silence was the only thing I'd ever known. My books were my safe space after another disgusting encounter with Mouth.

I glanced at Nikki. Her expression was distant, her pain just as evident. It killed me that my brother held her prisoner here. But what could I do? I was trapped, too, a prisoner of circumstances. Still, I had managed one small act of defiance: making an outgoing phone call to the number written on her shirt. All I could do was dial, set the phone down, and pray someone would come for her. I couldn't explain anything or stay on the line. Being deaf meant my actions were limited, but at least I had done something.

I caught Nikki's attention and signed to her, letting her know I'd get us some lunch. She gave me a weak nod, her shoulders slumped with the weight of her situation.

When I knocked on the door to be let out, I whispered a silent prayer of thanks that Mouth wasn't there. He'd left with Cross for a couple of days, giving me a much-needed break from his controlling and perverted presence.

The door opened, revealing Rat. His gaze was cold, predatory, lingering on Nikki in a way that made my stomach churn. Rat was the worst kind of person—dangerous and vile. I avoided his eyes and hurried to the kitchen.

If there was one thing Mouth ensured, it was that I had the essentials: clothes, food, and small comforts like books. I grabbed a couple of pre-made sandwiches and bottled water before heading back to the room.

When I returned, Rat was gone, and the knot of unease in my stomach tightened. Something wasn't right.

I opened the door cautiously, staying close to the frame—and froze. Rat was inside, pinning Nikki against the wall. His hands were on her, his intentions unmistakable.

Panic shot through me. I wanted to scream, but wasn't capable. My only choice was to act. I took a step back, intending to find help, but Rat noticed me. Before I could react, he grabbed me and threw me across the room.

Pain exploded as I slammed into the wall, my vision swimming. For a moment, I thought I'd pass out, but Nikki's terrified face snapped me back to focus. I couldn't let him hurt her. She didn't deserve this. If anyone did, it was me. I was already broken.

That's when I saw it—the knife I'd left on the tray to cut our sandwiches.

Dragging myself forward, I grabbed the knife with trembling hands. Somehow, I pushed myself upright and lunged at Rat, stabbing him in the back.

Even being deaf, I knew he roared in pain as he spun toward me, his fists pummeling me before I could strike again. Each blow fractured something inside me—bone, spirit, or both. The pain grew distant as I retreated into myself, sinking into a quiet, comforting darkness. If this was it, at least it was over. At least I'd be free.

When I came to, the room was a blur. Shapes moved around me, men shouting words I couldn't hear. Then I saw him.

The most beautiful brown eyes I had ever seen locked onto mine. His lips moved, forming words I couldn't understand, but the gentle touch of his hands on my face spoke volumes. In a world where everything was terrible, his touch felt grounding, reassuring.

That's the last thing I remembered before darkness claimed me again—those brown eyes, filled with something I couldn't quite name, anchoring me to this fragile thread of safety.

When I woke up in the hospital, those same brown eyes were there, watching over me. And for the first time in forever, I felt something I thought I'd lost: hope.

2

Six Weeks Later

"He's watching me sleep again."

I kept my eyes closed, pretending I hadn't noticed. Being deaf all my life, I've learned to rely on my other senses, and right now, I could feel his gaze—the soft, steady presence of those warm brown eyes watching me from his usual chair beside my bed.

Reader had been a constant in my life for the past six weeks. Always near, always supportive, and unfailingly kind.

And I didn't know what to make of this man.

I'd never had anyone care for me the way he did. The only other person who truly cared for me was my sister, Brooke. But when Flex claimed and married her, she had to leave the clubhouse. Ol' ladies were only allowed inside for special occasions, and that separation had been like losing a lifeline. Then there was Nikki. We'd grown close after surviving the nightmare with my brother, Cross, and his hostage games. We shared a bond that only trauma could forge.

Opening my eyes, I wasn't surprised to find Reader still watching me. As always, he reached for my glasses and slipped them onto my face so I could see, his thoughtfulness as natural as breathing.

"Are you hungry, Tildie?" Reader signed, his smile making his already handsome face somehow even more attractive.

Yes, this sweet, patient man had learned sign language just for me. Why he'd gone to that effort, I couldn't say. I figured I was his pity project—a broken girl he'd taken under his wing. There was no other reason a man like him would do the things he did for me.

I wasn't blind to how I looked. Pretty on the outside, but on the inside I saw the dirt, the scars, the weight of being defective. Reader deserved better than me.

He was handsome in a way that made it hard not to stare—chocolate brown hair that was perpetually messy, warm brown eyes that radiated kindness, and a muscular frame that seemed built to protect. He wasn't overly tall, maybe five-eight or five-nine, but he towered over my five-foot frame. He was everything Mouth wasn't.

Mouth, with his hulking frame, bald head, and ice-blue eyes, was the monster of my nightmares. The one who haunted my sleep. Reader, on the other hand, had become my dream of safety, a light in my darkness.

"I need to use the bathroom," I signed, relieved that my arm cast had come off a few days ago, making signing easier. My leg cast was another story. Doc said it would be another week before it came off. The beating I took had been brutal, but in the end, it was worth it to escape Mouth and the horrors of Cross's Fire Dragons MC.

"Okay, let's get you up," Reader signed back.

He gently pulled the covers back, careful to keep my nightgown in place, and slid his arms under me, lifting me with practiced ease. He carried me to the bathroom, where he had installed a safety railing by the toilet to help me balance.

Before my arm cast came off and my ribs began healing, I'd been stuck using a bedpan. It was humiliating, but Reader handled it like it was no big deal. Of course, Summer or Nikki usually helped me with that, but when Reader had to step in, he did so without hesitation or judgment.

He steadied me as I gripped the railing, then turned his back to give me privacy. He refused to leave the room, afraid I might fall, but I didn't mind. Reader had already seen me at my worst, taking care of me when I couldn't do it myself.

I tapped him on the shoulder when I was done, and he helped me wash my hands before scooping me back into his arms. My arms wrapped around his neck as I held on, breathing in the spicy warmth of his cologne.

Once he had me settled back in bed, sitting comfortably against the pillows, he touched my face lightly to get my attention.

"What's for breakfast today? Pancakes or French toast?" he signed, his smile soft and teasing.

I smiled back, my hands moving to answer. "That's a tough one. I think French toast with a side of bacon."

Reader's grin widened. "You got it, Tildie. I'll be right back."

I watched him leave, my heart twisting with an ache I didn't fully understand. I could only imagine what his voice sounded like—soft, soothing, like his presence.

I sighed and reached for the book on my nightstand, *Wuthering Heights*, one of Reader's favorites that he'd loaned to me. As I opened it, I allowed myself a moment of fantasy. If only I were more like Elizabeth Bennet—bold, confident, and worthy of a man like Reader.

But I wasn't Elizabeth, and Reader wasn't my Mr. Darcy.

Still, as I settled into the story, I couldn't help but hope that maybe, just maybe, I was wrong.

Tildie's smile could light up a room. She was beautiful, with shoulder-length black-as-night hair, a tiny nose, full lips, and the purest, biggest blue eyes I'd ever seen—eyes that seemed to take up most of her heart-shaped face. But it wasn't just her outward beauty that struck me. Tildie was equally beautiful on the inside, even if she didn't believe it.

She thought she was dirty and defective.

I knew this because I'd read her journal.

I still felt ashamed for doing it. It was among the books Nikki handed me that awful day when Tildie was beaten nearly to death. As I sat in the hospital, watching over her battered, unconscious body, I read the words she couldn't speak. Her pain spilled out in raw, heartbreaking detail. The anger that surged through me as I read was unlike anything I'd felt since the day my mom was murdered.

This beautiful soul—this innocent, resilient woman—had been mistreated her entire life. Worst of all was the torment inflicted by the man she called Mouth.

I vowed then and there to find him and end him. I would make sure Tildie never experienced that kind of pain or fear again.

I'd spend the rest of my life ensuring she was loved and cared for, that she'd never doubt her worth again.

I was going to be her Mr. Darcy.

I walked into the kitchen, where Silver sat talking with Jane. Silver was like a father to me, the person who'd saved me when I had no one else. Without him, I don't know where I'd be.

At fourteen, I'd gone to Juvenile Detention for killing the man who murdered my mom. Four long years later, I was released on my eighteenth birthday. Society wasn't kind to kids like me—I was homeless and starving when Silver found me. After hearing my story, he took pity on me, bringing me to the clubhouse and under his wing.

Jax hadn't been sure I had what it took to prospect, but Silver vouched for me, promising to take responsibility if I messed up. Thanks to him, I earned my patch last year. At twenty-three, I was a full-fledged member of the club.

"How's Tildie doing today?" Jane asked.

Jane was a petite, dark-haired woman in her fifties—Shay's mom, Silver's girlfriend, and the club's unofficial mother hen.

"She woke up smiling as usual," I said, a small smile tugging at my lips. "She's ready for French toast and bacon."

"I'll have it ready in a jiffy," Jane replied, heading for the stove.

Silver leaned back in his chair. "Who's sitting with Tildie while you're in Church? Shadow wants you at today's meeting, doesn't he?"

"Nikki's coming with Vampire. Probably Summer, too," I said.

"Just checking. You know I'll help however I can. She seems like a sweet girl—dealt a shitty hand, though."

"That's putting it lightly," I replied, the anger in my voice unmistakable.

Silver studied me for a moment. "Son, has she started opening up to you about what she's been through?"

I sighed heavily. "No, not really." Pausing, I ran a hand through my hair. "Silver, I did something I knew was wrong, but I don't regret it. It helped me understand her better so I could help her." I hesitated before confessing, "I read her journal."

Silver's eyes narrowed thoughtfully. "I get why you did it, but listen to me—Tildie's not going to be as understanding. That journal is her private space, and women take that shit seriously."

"Trust me, I know. I'm praying she never finds out. She'd feel betrayed," I said quietly. When I first started taking care of Tildie, I did it because we shared a connection—a love for losing ourselves in books. But as I've gotten to know her, my feelings have deepened.

I love her.

Jane set the tray of food in front of me. "Here you go, Reader."

"Thanks, Jane," I said, standing with the tray in hand. "I'd better get this to her before it gets cold."

Walking into Tildie's room, I saw Doc standing beside her bed.

"Morning, Reader," Doc greeted me as I set the tray on Tildie's lap and helped her get situated.

Doc turned to Tildie so she could read his lips. "Everything is healing as it should. I'll check on you again in a few days."

He looked at me as Tildie started eating. "I'm looking into a hearing specialist for her. As we discussed, I believe she might be able to speak and possibly hear with the help of a hearing aid. I'll let you know what I find out."

"Thanks, Doc. From what I can tell, she's never had proper medical care. I appreciate you doing this for her."

"She's been neglected long enough," Doc said, turning back to Tildie. She smiled and gave him a small wave goodbye.

I sat back down, letting Tildie know Nikki would be arriving soon. Opening the latest Stephen King novel, I began to read as Tildie quietly finished her breakfast.

I glanced at her every so often, watching her smile between bites. My heart ached with the hope that, one day, she'd see herself the way I saw her—strong, beautiful, and worthy of love.

They stole my most cherished possession.

My sweet Tildie.

I'm going to make each and every one of those bastards pay. Slowly. Painfully. But especially the one they call Reader. He'll suffer the most.

First, I need to get Tildie back. I miss her—my little girl. I know she misses me too. We've never been apart this long. She's hurt, vulnerable, and she needs me. That meth-head piece of shit, Rat, laid his filthy hands on her. He beat my sweet Tildie. Rat got off easy, dying before I could get to him. The other two men who stood by and let it happen didn't fare so well.

When I got back from that run with Cross and found her gone, I lost my mind. Watching the bar's security footage, seeing my girl dragged out, bloodied and broken, ignited a rage so deep it was like nothing I'd felt before. Not knowing where they had taken her only made it worse.

I started watching *The Devil's House* clubhouse. I followed their movements obsessively, and eventually, I got lucky. Reader—Tildie's wannabe savior—led me straight to her when he went to the hospital in Elkview.

I couldn't risk walking in myself. They'd notice me right away. So, I sent in one of the club sluts. She got close enough to find out what room Tildie was in. She told me everything she saw: how fragile my girl looked, how close she came to dying.

The thought of losing her...it shattered me.

But what sent me over the edge was finding out that Reader never left her side. That smug little prick stayed by her bedside, acting like he had some claim on her.

Then they moved her again—middle of the night, straight to their clubhouse.

Now, I watch and wait, perched in the trees like a predator stalking its prey. I've seen him. Reader. Wheeling Tildie outside in that damn chair, pretending to care for her. Acting like *I'm* the one who doesn't belong in her life.

When I saw her smile at him, my blood boiled. My sweet Tildie, giving *him* a smile meant for me. I wanted to rip him apart with my bare hands, to feel his life drain away as he realized he could never take my place.

He thinks he's protecting her. Taking care of her. But he'll learn soon enough.

Tildie is mine.

She has been since she was twelve.

And no one—*no one*—will ever take her from me.

3

I walked into the meeting room, taking a seat beside Kickstand. It wasn't often I was included in Sunday Church. The club held monthly meetings for all members, but weekly Church was reserved for officers and senior members.

"Hey, brother. How's Tildie?" Kickstand asked, his eyes glued to his laptop.

"Getting better every day," I replied.

"Glad to hear it."

Fuse strolled in, and moments later, Shadow slammed the gavel, signaling the start of the meeting.

"Kickstand, give us an update on the hacking attempts," Shadow said, his tone sharp.

"It's still an issue. I'm monitoring the firewalls constantly. Whoever their hacker is, they're good—but I'm better," Kickstand said with a smirk.

"Any idea who's behind it?" Vampire asked.

"Not yet. I've tracked the hacker to Pittsburgh, but every time I get close, they shift their IP address. Sooner or later, I'll catch a break."

"Keep at it," Shadow ordered. "In the meantime, don't let your guard down. We'll continue patrolling the grounds until this threat is neutralized."

Shadow shifted his gaze to me. "Reader, Doc says Tildie is doing much better. I see you've learned sign language to communicate with her. I don't want to push, but I'm betting she knows something about where Cross and Mouth have been hiding."

"She doesn't know their exact location," I began, "but she has been there."

Shadow's brow furrowed. "How do you know that? Did she tell you?"

I hesitated, taking a deep breath. "I'm going to tell you something in confidence. Only one other person knows this, and I don't want it getting out. Tildie has a journal. It was in the stack of books Nikki handed me the day everything went down. I read it. She can never know I did—it would break her to know anyone else knows what's in it. You need to promise me this stays in this room."

Shadow nodded, and the rest of the table gave their agreement.

"Mouth never leaves Tildie for more than a few days. If it's going to be longer, he takes her with him. Over the last year, they've moved around a lot. She wrote that they always arrive at night, so she never knows where she is. Being deaf, she can't hear anything to clue her in. But she always describes mountains and wildlife."

"West Virginia and the Pennsylvania border would be my guess," Fuse said.

"Sounds about right," Stonewall grumbled. "If he's been watching us, he'd stay close."

"Tildie's journal also mentioned Cross's vendetta against Shadow.

He blames you for his old man's death, and she's worried about how far he'll go with his grudge. Mouth drags her into everything—every scheme, every fight. But Tildie's the one who made the call that saved her and Nikki. She waited until the men were drunk and dialed the number on Nikki's shirt. Mouth never allowed her a phone."

"I owe her," Vampire said, his voice grim. "And I want to take care of Mouth so he can't bother her again. Do you think he'll come for her?"

"No doubt in my mind," I hissed, the anger boiling just beneath the surface. "Mouth's obsessed with her. He's been fixated on her since she was a child. He'll come for her. It's just a matter of time."

"Damn," Shadow muttered. "And what amazes me is that Tildie still smiles through all of it. How the hell does she do it?"

"She loses herself in books. It's how she copes. I used the same escape when I was a kid, so I recognized it right away. But deep down, she thinks she's ruined. That she's not worth anything."

"We need to change that," Viking said, echoed by grunts of agreement around the table.

"Tildie did ask for something," I said.

"What is it?" Shadow asked.

"She's worried about her sister Brooke, who was claimed by an abusive club member years ago. Brooke has a son, and Tildie wants us to check on her. She wrote down the name of the restaurant where Brooke works outside Philadelphia."

"I'll take care of it," Stonewall volunteered. "Let me know where the restaurant is, and I'll check on her in a few days. Need to shuffle some things at the tattoo shop first."

"Thanks, man. I'll get you the info," I said.

Shadow was about to continue when the front gate alarm blared, cutting him off. In seconds, we were out the door, guns in hand.

Gunshots rang out from the front gate, where Johnny and Black were returning fire on a black truck spinning out in retreat.

"What the fuck?" Shadow roared.

Domino sprinted up. "The truck drove to the gate, opened fire, then sped off."

"It's a distraction," Shadow and Viking growled in unison.

Another gunshot sounded from behind the clubhouse, followed by screaming.

"The women," Stonewall yelled, and we all took off toward the sound.

We rounded the corner to see a burly bald man backhanding Summer aside and then grabbing Ann by the neck. Mary lay on the ground, moaning in pain.

The man dropped Ann when he saw us coming, but Black was on him in a heartbeat, his fists flying. Stonewall and Lord pulled Black off the unconscious man.

Shadow knelt beside Mary, his face pale. "What's wrong, Kitten?" he asked softly, brushing her hair back as tears streamed down her face.

Summer knelt beside him. "He tried to take Mary while we were walking. Ann and I fought him off, but he dropped her. I think she's in labor. We need Doc."

"He's already on his way," Viking said.

Shadow carefully lifted Mary in his arms and carried her inside, followed by Summer and Viking. Stonewall and Lord dragged the unconscious man toward the basement.

"That man will wish for death when Shadow's done with him," Kickstand muttered as he walked off with Fuse, King, Vampire, and Soldier to investigate the breach.

I picked up the man's discarded gun, noting its condition. Once we reviewed the footage, we'd know exactly how he got in.

For now, I needed to see Tildie. She was safe in the clubhouse, but I wouldn't feel at ease until I saw her with my own eyes.

Doc rode up, and I knew we'd have a new baby in the club before the day was over. I just hoped everything would be okay. If anything happened to Mary or the baby, Shadow would lose it—and not a soul would be able to stop the carnage he would unleash.

Something was happening.

I watched Nikki stiffen, her movements tense, as she walked to the door. She poked her head out, speaking with someone briefly before plastering on a fake smile and returning to her seat.

I loved everyone here—they had been nothing but kind to me— but they treated me with kid gloves, like I was some fragile child. The one thing I've never been allowed to be is a child, so I wish they wouldn't shield me. I've been handling bad situations my entire life.

Reader walked in, and my heart skipped when his eyes met mine. Those deep brown orbs could pull me in, make me forget everything else. He smiled at me in greeting before turning to Nikki. They spoke quietly for a moment before Nikki turned, ensuring I could see her face clearly.

"Bye, Tildie," she said, smiling. "I'll see you later, and I'll bring that book I promised."

She leaned in to kiss my cheek before leaving the room.

As soon as the door closed, I looked at Reader. "What's going on? Don't lie to me."

Reader sighed heavily, his broad shoulders slumping slightly. "There was an attack on the clubhouse. Mary was hurt, and it triggered her labor. Doc is with her now."

"Oh no," I signed, my hands trembling. "Was it Cross?"

My brother's obsession with Shadow had spiraled out of control. At this point, I believed only death would put an end to it. Cross couldn't understand that our dad brought everything on himself. Both our dad and Jax, Shadow's father, had died that night.

"We're not sure yet, but we'll find out," Reader replied, his expression determined.

"I hope Mary will be okay," I signed. Mary had been so kind and welcoming to me since I arrived.

Reader reached out, squeezing my hand gently. He paused, tilting his head as though listening for something, then his face broke into a big smile. "I hear a baby crying. Our newest club member has arrived. Let me check."

He rose from his chair and stepped into the hall. My room was right next to the infirmary, so he wasn't gone long—maybe five minutes—before he returned.

"Marilyn Ruth Kelley has arrived," he announced, grinning. "Mother and daughter are both doing fine."

Relief swept over me, and I clutched my hands to my chest. "I'm so glad," I signed.

But the momentary relief was fleeting. The weight of being Cross's sister pressed down on me again. I couldn't help but feel responsible for his actions, even though he'd never truly been a brother to me. At least my dad had tried to protect me from Mouth, though it didn't do much good. When Dad was killed, I had just turned sixteen. Cross handed me over to Mouth like I was nothing.

I shuddered at the memory.

"Are you cold?" Reader asked, reaching for a blanket.

I grabbed his hand, stopping him. "No, I'm fine," I signed quickly.

Reader's gaze softened. "I have some good news for you," he signed. "Stonewall is going to check on your sister this week."

My heart swelled with gratitude. "I'm so happy," I signed back. "I've been so worried. The last time I saw Brooke, she told me Flex was getting worse. I'm scared for her and her son, Gael. He's only four."

Reader smiled reassuringly. "If there's one guy you can count on, it's Stonewall. He'll do a thorough check." He paused, his hands moving fluidly as he asked, "Do you want to go to the kitchen for lunch today? Get out of this room for a bit?"

I marveled at how natural Reader was with signing. His movements were smooth and precise, something I never thought I'd experience with someone outside the world of silence. Reader was the first person I'd met who could sign, and it made me feel normal for once.

"Yes, I'd like that," I signed, a genuine smile spreading across my face.

Reader wheeled the chair over, lifting me with practiced ease and settling me gently into the seat. He tucked a blanket over my lap, then crouched in front of me, a soft smile playing on his lips.

"Let's get you some lunch, beautiful."

Heat rose to my cheeks, and I felt a blush spread across my face. It was the first time Reader had called me beautiful. For a brief moment, a glimmer of longing surfaced, but I quickly squashed it down.

If life had taught me anything, it was not to get my hopes up. Disappointment was inevitable, and letting myself dream about Reader would only lead to more sadness.

So, I plastered on a smile as he wheeled me into the hallway, determined to keep it there until I was alone.

Cross is one stupid motherfucker! I warned him not to try to grab Shadow's ol' lady, especially on a Sunday when almost all the members were at the clubhouse for their Sunday bike run. But did he fucking listen?

Fuck no.

Now getting in will be tens times harder. It took a month to find a way around the fence. Now, it was all for nothing, thanks to Cross.

Cross isn't fit to run this club. He sure as hell ain't his old man. Cross has no control and doesn't think before he acts. He wanted to get the bitch before she popped that kid out. His only focus is on making Shadow suffer.

But I want my little girl, and now I'll have to wait longer before I can get Tildie. Security around the clubhouse will be fucking tighter than it has been.

Goddammit!

I miss holding Tildie and playing with her.

I reached down, adjusting my cock, which grew at thoughts of my sweetie and what we shared. I signaled one of the club sluts to come to me. "Suck me off," I growled, leaning my head back, letting my mind fill with images of my Tildie. I hope she'll understand why I had to use the club slut without her near me. My little girl was so sensitive, and I didn't want to hurt her. The sluts didn't compare to my little girl. These bitches were just pussy.

I only love my little Matilda.

4

I watched Tildie as she sat in her wheelchair reading. I wheeled her outside today for some sunshine and fresh air. I've decided it's time to let Tildie know how I feel about her. I knew I would have to go slow, and the physical part of our relationship would take time. Tildie has only been shown that being intimate hurts and is dirty, courtesy of that perverted prick Mouth.

But I was a patient man. I'm not like a lot of men who only think about getting their dick wet. I'm no virgin, but I'm not overly experienced, either. In order to have sex with a woman, I need some connection, something other than her physical appearance, to draw me into being intimate. And I've rarely found that and never as deep as the connection I feel with Tildie.

Something about her draws me in, like meeting her was meant to happen.

I think I see things differently than most men, maybe because of how I grew up. My mom was a prostitute, but I never judged her for that. She did everything she could to be a good mom to me—the best she knew how to be. I never went without what I needed: food, clothes, and most importantly, love and attention.

She homeschooled me, teaching me to read, and from there, I devoured books, losing myself in the fantasies they created. Books became my escape, especially when I was hiding in the closet while her johns were in the apartment. That was my reality until I was old enough to leave and only return when they were gone.

One time, though, I came back too late. That day changed everything.

I shook the memory away, pushing it into the recesses of my mind. Today wasn't about the past. It was about the beautiful woman sitting in front of me.

Tildie.

I planned to start slow, with small touches and quiet moments, building her trust one step at a time. I reached across the table and took her hand gently, feeling the warmth of her skin as her wide, surprised eyes met mine. "Can I get you anything?" I asked, keeping my tone light. I knew she was skittish, and patience was key. My thumb brushed over her fingers, a subtle touch meant to soothe, before I let go.

Her cheeks turned the prettiest shade of pink as she lowered her eyes, shyly glancing back up at me. "No, I'm good. I just can't wait to get my cast off this week. I feel like such a burden, taking up all your time."

I leaned closer, locking onto those deep blue eyes that held more pain than anyone should ever carry. "Tildie, you are not a burden. There's nowhere I'd rather be than right here with you. Don't ever think otherwise. Got me?"

She lowered her gaze again, and I reached out, brushing my fingers lightly along the side of her face, coaxing her to look at me. "Got me?" I repeated softly.

Her smile lit up the day, rivaling the sun itself. "Yes, I got you," she signed, her face still flushed.

"When you get your cast off," I said, leaning back slightly, "I'm taking you to Elkview. There's a bookstore there with thousands of used books—a book lover's dream."

Her face lit up even more, her excitement unmistakable. I knew from reading her journal how much she loved books, how Mouth had kept her from going anywhere, always controlling what she could have or do.

She clapped her hands together, her grin spreading wide. "I would love that! How exciting to explore so many books. I can't wait."

"Me either," I said honestly. "I've been there plenty of times, but I've never had anyone to share it with—someone who appreciates how amazing it is."

I glanced at my watch and sighed. "I have to take you back inside. I've got a meeting. Summer will sit with you in the common room if you need anything and you can visit." Shadow had called the meeting to finish what we'd started yesterday before everything went sideways.

"Okay," she signed. Then, after a moment's hesitation, she added, "Can you bring me some more books when you come back?"

"Of course. Anything in particular?"

"Nope. Whatever you have is fine."

She said that, but I knew better. Tildie loved romance, all kinds, so I'd been picking up books for her whenever I went out. I'd mix them in with the ones I already had, surprising her with new stories to escape into.

I pushed her wheelchair back inside, guiding her toward the table where Summer sat chatting with Lettie and Joe. After making sure Tildie had her notebook and pen within reach, I leaned down, brushing my hand gently against her face.

"I'll be back in an hour or so," I told her, smiling softly.

Her eyes lingered on mine as I straightened and walked away. I could feel the knowing looks from the women at the table. That was fine by me.

I wanted everyone to know one thing:

I love Tildie.

My mind was spinning. There was no mistaking it—Reader was interested in me.

Or so it seemed.

I wanted to believe it so badly, but maybe I was reading too much into his touches and words. Still, he planned to take me places once my cast was off. That had to mean he wanted to spend time with me. Right?

And not just anywhere—a massive bookstore.

I had dreamed of visiting a bookstore my entire life.

With Mouth, I wasn't allowed such luxuries. He'd make me look up the books I wanted online, then pick them up for me. I was never allowed outside the clubhouse unless it was with him, and even then, it was always to a new location.

Before Mouth, my dad kept us kids locked away, homeschooled by the club women. He believed public schools were a government brainwashing tool, so we were sheltered from the outside world. On the rare occasions when Dad went on runs, the club women would sneak us out to get what we needed—usually a trip to Walmart. But even that felt like an adventure to Brooke and me.

Cross got more freedom as he got older, but Brooke and I weren't so lucky. None of our mothers stuck around; they were all club women, dismissed by Dad as being "worthless." That left us at his mercy—and later, at Cross's.

Lettie's touch on my hand pulled me from my thoughts. I looked up as she smiled at me, her lips forming the words slowly so I could read them. "Reader is into you."

I liked Lettie. She didn't treat me like I was fragile. Last week, she gave me a haircut, styled it, and even gave me my first pedicure and manicure. Before that, I'd always cut my own hair. When I told her that, she'd made a dramatic horror face and declared, "Never again."

I pulled out my notebook and wrote, "He's just being nice."

Lettie grabbed the notebook and scribbled in bold letters, *Bullshit,* followed by a smiley face.

Joe leaned over and wrote, *I second that,* adding a wink for good measure. Summer grinned at me, giving a thumbs-up in agreement.

I sighed and wrote back, "We'll see. Men are fickle."

Growing up in a motorcycle clubhouse had taught me that men were rarely loyal to one woman. The men kept the club women busy, whether or not they had an ol' lady. Flex always cheated on Brooke, but she didn't care—it kept him away from her.

Even Mouth, if I were on my period, he would bring a club woman into my bedroom. He would blindfold her and have sex in front of me. I was forced to sit naked and watch while he kept his eyes on me the whole time. It was so awful, and I wanted to know why he did it. His answer: It wasn't cheating if I was part of it, and he only used the club woman as a hole until my bleeding stopped. Mouth couldn't stomach period blood.

Which made me wish for a longer period.

Summer caught my attention. "You've been around the wrong kind of men. Reader and the men here are different. You'll see," she said slowly, her words clear and deliberate for me to read.

I smiled at her but didn't respond. The women moved on, chatting among themselves. Summer might be right—the men here were different. But even if Reader felt something for me now, it would change when he discovered how ruined I was.

Being deaf was hard enough. Add to that the things Mouth did to me, starting when I was just a girl, and I didn't know if I could ever be normal.

I tried to follow their conversation, but they spoke too quickly, so I opened my book and escaped into its pages.

Until I saw Reader walk in.

Books in hand, he was intercepted by a curvy brunette I recognized as a club girl. She leaned in, whispering something in his ear, her hand resting on his chest. He smiled politely and shook his head before stepping away from her.

Our eyes met, and guilt flickered in his expression, like he knew I'd seen the interaction. He shouldn't feel bad—I had no claim on him. I smiled at him, brushing it off, and saw the relief on his face as he made his way to the table.

But doubt had already crept in. Was he sleeping with her? She was beautiful, confident, and normal—everything I wasn't.

As much as I craved someone like Reader in my life, doubt buried itself deep, a thorn pressing against my fragile hope. I couldn't risk getting hurt. Keeping my heart guarded was the only way to protect myself.

Lettie slid my notebook back to me as she stood, a knowing smile on her lips. I glanced down to see what she had written:

I see your mind working, young lady. You're reading too much into that little scene. Reader has no interest in Lexi—he never has. You're a beautiful, sweet person, and you need to realize that. Reader already has.

The words hit me like a wave, and tears threatened to spill. I wanted to believe her. I *wanted* to believe Reader could see me that way. But a lifetime of being told otherwise made it hard to accept.

I closed the notebook quickly as Reader bent down to talk to me. Plastering on a smile, I hid the storm inside as he greeted me with that warm, comforting presence I craved so much.

5

I watched as **Shadow took his seat at the** head of the table. He looked exhausted, dark circles shadowing his eyes.

"Congratulations on your baby girl," Lord said, breaking the silence. The others quickly joined in with their congratulations.

"Thanks," Shadow said, his expression softening. "She's a beauty and looks just like her mother."

"You know what this means, don't you, Shadow?" Fuse smirked. "Should we sign the marriage contract now or later?"

"No fucking way my Marilyn ends up with Preston," Shadow chuckled, shaking his head. "At least not if he's anything like you."

"You can't stop destiny," Fuse teased, his grin widening.

Shadow's demeanor hardened instantly. "Let's get started. Is that bastard still alive?"

"Barely," Viking replied, his tone grim. "After Black had his turn, and then I went at him for backhanding Summer, he's in rough shape but still breathing."

I wasn't surprised Viking had sought retribution. Summer being pregnant made the hit she took even more unforgivable.

"Good," Shadow growled. "I'll finish him off—slowly. Did he say who sent him to take Mary? And how the fuck did they get inside?"

"He was sent by Cross," Vampire said, his voice steady. "Cross promised him a patch if he delivered Mary. They breached the perimeter near a corner fence close to your house. Dug a hole underneath it. But they didn't think it through. There's no way he could've gotten Mary out the same way."

Kickstand spun his laptop around to show Shadow the footage.

"Cross isn't exactly known for his brains," Shadow muttered, slamming his fist on the table. "I want that motherfucker found. No more waiting. No more playing games. We do whatever it takes to get him."

"Got it, Shadow," Stonewall said, his jaw tightening. "I want him as much as you do. If we don't find him, he'll eventually succeed—and we can't let that happen."

Shadow turned to me. "Reader, I know Tildie might think she doesn't know anything, but I need you to pick her brain. And Stonewall, when you check on Brooke, stay awhile and watch. If you can follow Flex, it might lead us to Cross."

"I'll talk to Tildie," I assured him. "She trusts me enough now to open up more. And she has no love for her brother."

Shadow's attention shifted. "Next, how do we stop another breach like this one?"

"Vampire and I have a plan," Kickstand said. "We'll install an underground security system around the fence line. It's not cheap, but it'll alert us to any attempts like yesterday."

"I don't care about the cost," Shadow replied. "And I want the same system installed around my house."

"Consider it done," Kickstand said with a nod.

"Is Mary doing okay?" Stonewall asked.

Shadow's face softened again. "Yeah. The fall triggered her labor, and it scared the hell out of both of us since she wasn't due for another two weeks. But Doc says she and the baby are fine. He's staying at my house for the next few days to keep an eye on them. Feel free to stop by to see Mary and Marilyn."

"It was nice of you to name her after your mothers," Stonewall said, looking thoughtful. "I'll stop by before I leave for Philadelphia."

"Thanks, brother," Shadow said, his tone sincere. "She'd love to see you." He straightened. "Let's move on. Runner, Poison, Black, and Silver are headed to Florida later this month. Fuse, get the trip planned and send it to Silver by the end of the week."

"On it," Fuse said.

"And one more thing about the sweet butts," Shadow continued. "After the shit with Carla, Wanda, and now Jen, I've decided not to replace them. We still have four left, and they'll have to do. I'll bring it up at the next monthly meeting, but with more ol' ladies joining, having those women around creates a toxic environment. I just wanted to touch base on that."

Shadow slammed the gavel down, dismissing the meeting. As he left, I hurried to my room, grabbing a handful of books for Tildie. I thought I was a fast reader, but she put me to shame.

Walking into the common room, I was intercepted by Lexi with her usual proposition. I'd told her I wasn't interested, but she still tried. I hated to be an ass, but I might have to be—especially after I saw Tildie watching. Her trust was fragile, and I wouldn't risk losing it over Lexi.

Tildie smiled at me, but the relief I felt didn't last long. Her smile didn't reach her eyes, and I knew Lexi's approach had planted doubts in her mind.

I'd be having a talk with Lexi.

For now, honesty was the best approach. I crouched beside Tildie, gently tilting her chin up so she had to look at me. Then I signed, "What you saw was Lexi propositioning me. She does it all the time, but I've never been interested in what she offers. I don't sleep with the club women. I want you to know that."

Tildie started to sign back, but I stopped her. "I know you'll say it doesn't matter, but it does. I need you to know."

She studied me for a moment, then gave me one of her

breathtaking smiles. "Thank you, Reader."

"Call me Travis," I signed. "That's my real name—Travis Baylor."

Her eyes widened slightly, and her smile softened. "Thank you, Travis."

"Are you ready for your daily walk?" I asked. Doc wanted her to walk with crutches every day to exercise her good leg and prevent blood clots.

"Yes, I need my crutches," she signed.

"I'll grab them and be right back. Let's walk outside today."

As I left to fetch her crutches, I couldn't help but feel a sense of hope. Tildie was letting me in, and I'd do whatever it took to prove to her that I deserved to be there.

I had to pinch myself to make sure I wasn't dreaming.

How did I get so lucky to find someone like Reader—or Travis, as he wants me to call him now? He is everything I've ever fantasized about, my prince charming come to life.

But I know, eventually, I'll have to tell him my dirty secret.

Someone as good as Travis deserves honesty. I can't let him be deceived by who he thinks I am. He's been nothing but honest with me, and I owe him the same.

The wheelchair stopped, pulling me out of my thoughts. Travis was there, steady and dependable as always, helping me stand and positioning my crutches under my arms. His hands stayed on me, holding me securely until I was stable. Only then did he let go, walking beside me as I slowly made my way down the path.

Because I had to focus on keeping my balance, we couldn't communicate. But his presence was enough. Comforting. Steady. Safe.

And then there was the way he looked.

The tight blue jeans that hugged his muscular frame, the blue t-shirt under his club cut that fit perfectly, and those black boots. I wanted to run my hands through his already messy brown hair.

The thought startled me. I've never wanted to touch a man before —not like this. Mouth had destroyed that part of me. Or so I thought.

Travis's hand on my shoulder stopped me, and I realized we had reached the bench at the end of the path. It was time to rest before heading back. He helped me sit down and get comfortable, his every movement careful and considerate.

"What had you thinking so hard?" he asked, his warm eyes watching me closely.

I blushed, unable to stop myself from signing, "How lucky I am to have you."

I hadn't meant to say it, but it was the truth.

Travis's smile was soft and full of something I couldn't quite name as he pulled me close. His arms wrapped around me, his hands holding me gently against his chest. The warmth of his embrace felt so good, so safe, that I didn't resist.

When his fingers threaded through my hair, tilting my head back so I could see his face, my breath caught. Then, his lips brushed mine —a soft, barely-there kiss that left me frozen in place.

But suddenly, Travis pulled back, his expression shifting. He signed quickly, "We need to head back. I'll explain later."

Before I could respond, he scooped me up in his arms, leaving my crutches by the bench as he jogged back to my wheelchair. He placed me in it carefully, wheeling me back inside.

Once we were safely indoors, Travis pulled out his phone and made a call. His spoke quickly, his body tense in a way I wasn't used to seeing.

When he ended the call, he turned to me, his expression serious. "I heard a loud crash in the woods behind the fence. I'm not sure what it was, but I didn't want to take any chances. I wanted to get you inside and safe before checking it out."

"Will you be alright here while I go investigate?" he asked, his hands moving fluidly as he signed.

"Yes," I signed back. "Go do what you need to do."

Before leaving, he bent down and pressed a quick kiss to my cheek. My fingers instinctively touched the spot as I watched him walk out the door.

Sighing, I closed my eyes and let the moment sink in. This—being close to him, feeling cared for—was something I'd cherish. Because deep down, I feared that once I told him the truth about Mouth, moments like this would disappear.

A light touch on my hand brought me back to the present. I opened my eyes to find Ann sitting at the table beside me. She smiled warmly, and I returned the gesture, grateful for the distraction as we visited and waited for Travis to return.

6

I met Shadow, Black, and Viking out front, and we walked to the bench where it happened. "We were sitting here when I heard a loud crash, like something hitting the ground, followed by the sound of someone rushing toward us from behind the fence. I think it was Mouth," I told them, my voice steady despite the anger festering beneath the surface.

Vampire and Stonewall appeared on the other side of the fence, their expressions grim.

"There was definitely someone back here," Vampire confirmed. "The damage to the brush and the footprints in the dirt make that clear."

Shadow turned to me, his dark eyes sharp. "Why do you think it was Mouth?"

"Because of what I was doing before it happened," I said, glancing toward the bench. "I was hugging Tildie, and I had just kissed her. Mouth is obsessed with her—seeing something like that would drive him over the edge."

"That would mean he's watching, waiting for a chance to grab her," Viking said, voicing the fear I already had.

"Why didn't he claim her with a property patch if he's so obsessed?" Vampire asked, his tone curious but laced with disgust.

"Their club is old school," I explained. "To claim an old lady, it has to be done in front of the entire club—with the couple having sex. According to what Tildie wrote, Mouth refused to do that because he didn't want anyone seeing her that way. He's possessive to the point of insanity. That's why I think he rushed the fence—watching me touch Tildie must have infuriated him."

Shadow nodded, his jaw tight. "I think you're right. Only someone overcome with rage would give themselves away like that. How long until the new security system is up?" He looked at Vampire.

"The equipment will be here in a few days. Installation will take another few days after that," Vampire replied.

"Until then, we need to stay vigilant," Shadow said firmly. "I know it's boring as fuck, but I want phones put away and foot patrols around the perimeter. With a property this size, it's hard to cover every inch, but we have to try. I'll send an email updating everyone." He ran a hand through his dark hair before rubbing his face, the strain evident.

"I'm going to stay with Tildie as much as possible," I said, gripping her crutches tightly. "I'll make sure she's never alone."

"You let us know if you need any help," Vampire said, his voice resolute. "We vowed to protect that girl, and we will." His lips twitched into a small smile. "Looks like she'll be our next ol' lady."

"I hope so," I admitted, the thought warming me despite the circumstances. "But Mouth did a number on Tildie. I need to take it slow with her."

"You're the right man for her," Black said confidently. "Anyone can see that."

"We're going to search the area some more," Vampire added. "If we find anything else, we'll let you know." He and Stonewall disappeared into the brush, their boots crunching against the forest floor.

"I need to get back to Tildie," I said, turning toward the clubhouse.

I hated knowing Mouth had been watching us, hated that I hadn't picked up on it sooner. The idea of his eyes on her made my skin crawl. He had no right to even look at her. From now on, I'd stay with her at night. Even though the chances of someone getting inside were slim, I wouldn't rest knowing she was alone.

I'll protect Tildie with my life.

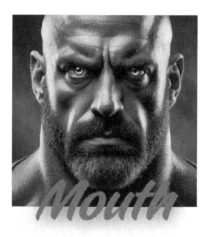

How could she do it?

My little girl let another man hug her!

Kiss her!

My rage burned at seeing that little fucker touch Tildie, causing me to give up my location. I wanted to rip that fence down with my bare hands, kill Reader, and take back Tildie.

No other man was allowed to touch her that way but me. She

was mine, *and she let him*! I have never had to punish my sweet girl, but when I got her back, I would teach her a lesson she won't forget.

When I'm done, she'll never forget who she belongs to again.

I know they are brainwashing Tildie, turning her against me. Just like her bitch of a sister used to do, telling her shit and running to their old man, telling him I was touching Tildie. He had a soft spot for his kids and would tell me to back off. I have only ever loved and cared for the sweet girl. But I fixed Brooke by making sure Flex claimed her and got her out of the clubhouse so she couldn't snitch.

And then, once their dad Cruise was killed, Cross gave me control of Tildie for my vote to replace Cruise as prez of the club. That was the only way he was getting my vote. And once I had full control over Tildie, I made her mine in every way.

Tildie was always meant to be mine. From the first time I laid eyes on her as a little girl, I knew when she looked up at me with those big blue eyes on that heart-shaped face, so small and pretty. She needed taking care of, and I'd be the one to do it. Only me.

I would have to find a way to watch now that they knew I was there. Hopefully, the hacker we have working on breaking their security will be successful, but until then, I'll watch the roads. Tildie has to leave at some point, and I'll be waiting.

7

He was climbing into bed with me again. I felt his breath on my neck as he put his lips there and started moving his hands down my body. I stiffened, and inside, I was screaming. With Brooke gone, there was no one to stop him.

Why me?

Would this never end?

Tears slid down my cheeks as his hand moved under my nightgown. I pushed at him, wanting him to stop, but he only held me tighter. His big hands touched what he had no right to touch. His body moved, and I could feel that part of him that terrified me. I sobbed harder, hoping he would stop.

I woke with a start, my heart racing so fast it felt like it might burst.

Arms came around me, and instinctively, I started to fight—until I saw Travis. His concerned eyes met mine, grounding me back into reality.

I'd been having a nightmare, and Travis must have woken me. He pulled me close, leaning back against the pillows with me cradled in his arms. He didn't say anything, just held me, letting me settle and come back to myself.

Travis was staying in my room tonight, sleeping on a cot in the corner. He said he felt better knowing I was protected around the clock, and I had to admit, I felt better too.

After a while, he shifted so he could look at me. "Do you want to talk about it?"

I couldn't—not yet. Shaking my head, I avoided his gaze.

"That's okay," he said, tenderly touching my face. "But if you ever need to talk, I'm always here."

"Thank you," I signed, managing a small smile.

Travis brought my hand to his lips, brushing a gentle kiss across my knuckles before releasing it. "You're safe now, Tildie," he said, his eyes promising me. "No one will ever hurt you again. I swear."

"I believe you," I signed back.

And I did. I trusted Travis completely. I knew he would never hurt me or let anyone else hurt me either.

He moved off the bed, helping me into a sitting position and turning on the bedside lamp before handing me a glass of water. That's when I noticed he was only wearing sweatpants.

Hard muscle. Every inch of him was solid strength.

I couldn't stop staring. When my gaze finally flicked up to meet his, my cheeks burned with embarrassment.

He caught me ogling him.

Travis smirked, but he looked away, sparing me the humiliation of lingering on the moment. He pulled on a t-shirt, the fabric stretching over his broad chest, before turning back to me. "Do you need the bathroom?" he asked.

"No, I'm good," I signed, reaching for my book and glasses. "I think I'll read until I get tired again."

Travis sat on the edge of the bed, his weight sinking the mattress slightly. "Tildie, I want you to know you can tell me anything. And nothing you say will ever change how I feel about you. When you're ready, I'm here."

His words were a lifeline, steady and sincere.

He squeezed my hand before standing and heading into the bathroom, giving me a moment to collect myself.

But he's wrong.

No man would want a girl who's been used and dirtied.

Even if he could accept me, I wasn't sure I could ever have a normal relationship. Mouth had taken that from me.

I wished Brooke were here. I could almost hear her telling me to try, to give Travis a chance. She would tell me I deserved happiness. Maybe, when I built up the courage, I'd finally tell him everything.

Travis came back out of the bathroom, his expression soft as he smiled at me. He lay down on the cot and opened a book, the sight of him so familiar and comforting that I felt the tension in my chest loosen.

I smiled back, opening my own book. At this moment I felt safe and content.

As I settled into the story, I prayed silently that this feeling would never end.

Finally, God had answered my prayers and sent me Travis. Surely He wouldn't be so cruel as to take him away.

I pretended to read, but my mind was on Tildie.

Tonight, for the first time, I'd heard her voice.

It wasn't the way I'd imagined, though. Her whimpers and cries had pulled me from sleep, raw and strangled with fear. Realizing it was Tildie, I'd rushed to her side, finding her trembling and terrified.

I knew the nightmare was about Mouth and the horrors that sick fuck inflicted on her. Carefully, I woke her, speaking softly and holding her until she calmed.

The question haunted me: why hadn't anyone stopped Mouth?

From what I'd gathered through her journal, aside from her sister Brooke, no one had made much effort to protect her. The thought boiled my blood. But I was here now, and I'd make damn sure she never suffered from that bastard's touch again.

I guess I had my mom to thank for my own survival. She cared enough to hide me, never letting her johns know I existed. When I was a kid, I used to hate being shoved into that dark closet. But now, I understood why she did it. She knew there were sick, twisted men out there, and she was protecting me.

I only wish I could've protected her.

I'd been too late to save her, but I'd avenged her. Her killer was six feet under.

And soon, Mouth would join him.

I glanced at Tildie; her face bathed in the soft light of the bedside lamp. She was lost in the pages of a romance novel I'd picked up for her at the used bookstore. A wistful smile tugged at her lips, and my chest tightened at the sight.

Like me, reading calmed her. It gave her an escape, a way to forget for a little while.

But I couldn't forget the way she'd let me hold her after the nightmare. How she'd clung to me, finding comfort in my arms. She was starting to trust me, becoming more comfortable around me.

I wanted to hold her longer, to protect her from everything that haunted her. But I knew she needed space, time to recover in her own way. She needed to read, to find solace in her books.

Plus, holding Tildie reminded me that she is very much a woman with luscious curves for someone her size, and my dick noticed. I could control myself. That wasn't the issue. I just didn't want to scare her with my arousal, so I got out of bed and went to the bathroom to let my body cool down.

She read for another half hour before closing the book with a soft thud. The sound drew my attention, and I looked over as she set it on the table.

"I think I can sleep now," she signed, her movements slow and deliberate.

I stood and helped her settle back into bed, making sure she was comfortable.

"Goodnight, Tildie," I said, leaning down to press a kiss to her cheek.

Her eyes flickered with something I couldn't quite place before I turned off the lamp and returned to my cot in the corner.

It was a long time before I fell asleep.

8

My cast comes off today, and I couldn't be more excited.

At last, I'll have more mobility and won't be so dependent on Travis and Nikki. Doc warned me there would still be some swelling, and I'd need to keep elevating my leg. It would take a few weeks before I was back to one hundred percent. But none of that mattered—I was ready to be free of the cast.

And I could finally take a real bath.

Summer had been helping me every few days, but keeping the cast dry made it challenging. I couldn't wait to soak in warm water without worrying about it.

Travis lifted me from my chair and onto the table, propping pillows behind me so I could sit comfortably. He adjusted the hem of my blue sundress, his hands gentle but precise. "You good?" he asked, his gaze searching mine.

"Yes, perfect," I signed, smiling.

I loved wearing pretty sundresses. Mouth never let me wear anything that didn't completely cover my body. The clothes I'd been wearing since arriving here were different—new, well-fitting, and a reflection of who I wanted to be, not who I had been forced to be.

Doc walked in carrying what looked like a miniature saw. His dark hair was thick, his green eyes sharp yet kind. Muscular and dressed in jeans, a t-shirt, and boots, he looked more like a biker than a doctor. When I first saw him at the hospital, wearing his cut, I couldn't believe he was a real doctor.

But he was, and a good one at that. He cared deeply, far more than any of the doctors that treated me. I was grateful to have him overseeing my recovery.

"You ready to get this thing off?" Doc asked, pointing to my cast and speaking slowly so I could read his lips.

I grabbed my notebook and wrote in bold letters, *YES*, holding it up for him to see. I could tell he chuckled and it made me smile.

"This saw won't cut you," Doc explained, holding it up. "It moves side to side, so it won't penetrate the skin. You might feel some tingling and warmth, but that's normal. Ready?"

I nodded, and Doc got to work.

Travis took my hand, his thumb brushing over mine as the saw buzzed to life. The sound was a little unnerving, but having Travis there calmed me.

Five minutes later, the cast was off. My leg felt strange—lighter, weaker—but it was a relief to be free of the bulk.

Doc handed me a sheet of paper. "These are your aftercare instructions. You'll still need help for a couple of weeks, and don't overdo it," he said firmly.

Travis took the paper, scanning it. "I'll make sure she follows everything," he said, signing as he spoke so I could follow.

Doc smiled. "I have no doubt you will, Reader." He turned back to me. "I want to see you next week to check your progress. Make sure to do the exercises on the list—they're critical for your recovery."

I gave him a thumbs-up, letting him know I understood.

Doc patted my leg lightly. "See you next week, Tildie," he said before leaving the room.

Travis scooped me up again, setting me gently in the wheelchair. Then he leaned down until we were eye level.

"Are you ready for some lunch?"

I smiled. "I need the bathroom first, and then lunch sounds great," I signed.

Travis grinned. "Bathroom it is," he said, moving behind the chair to push me into my room.

Once inside, he lifted me from the chair and carried me into the bathroom, helping me stand while holding onto the railings. I tested putting a little weight on my leg and was relieved to find it didn't hurt. Still, I knew I needed to take it slow.

Travis turned his back to give me privacy, waiting until I tapped his shoulder to let him know I was done. Even though he probably already knew, he never rushed me. He helped me wash my hands and carried me back to the chair.

"Let's go eat," he signed, pushing me toward the kitchen.

As we moved through the hallway, a thought struck me—I didn't know much about Travis Baylor, the man who had so quickly become my protector and my safe haven.

I wanted to know everything about him.

But first, I would tell him everything about me.

And pray he'd still want to let me into his world afterward.

9

I watched as Tildie cuddled baby Marilyn, her delicate hands cradling the tiny girl close. Her soft smile as she looked down at the baby made my chest tighten. Tildie would make an amazing mother; she had such a kind and nurturing heart.

When Tildie glanced up at me, her blue eyes shimmering with unspoken longing, I couldn't help but smile back and wink at her. The pretty blush that spread across her cheeks made my grin widen.

I would give Tildie as many children as she wanted—someday. But first, I needed to help her tear down the walls she had built around her heart.

It had been about a week since her cast came off, and she was already making incredible progress. She'd ditched the wheelchair and was now using crutches to get around. At the pace she was going, I had no doubt she'd be walking on her own in no time. She barely needed help anymore, though I still slept in her room at night.

It wasn't just about her safety anymore.

She had nightmares almost every night, and I wanted to be there to comfort her when they came. Once she opened up to me, I planned to suggest seeing a therapist. She needed someone who could help her work through the trauma of her past—and as much as I cared for her, I wasn't equipped to give her the professional help she deserved.

"Tildie's making great progress," Shadow said, sliding onto the barstool beside me.

"Yeah," I said, nodding. "She's stronger than people think."

Shadow leaned back, his gaze thoughtful. "She is. But because she's so small, it's easy to overlook. Have you thought about what happens once she's healed?"

"What do you mean?"

"Well," Shadow began, "Tildie can stay here as long as she wants. But I think it's worth asking her what *she* wants."

"Tildie will be staying here," I said confidently. "I know she wants to, and I need to talk to her about it. I'd hoped to take her out of the clubhouse, romance her a little. But with Mouth lurking, I can't risk it."

Shadow nodded, his expression steady. Few people I trusted with personal conversations, but Shadow was one of them. He'd been there for me when I was prospecting, cutting through the bullshit and giving it to me straight.

"Where's one place you'd like to take her?" he asked.

"There's a bookstore in Elkview I know she'd love," I said without hesitation. "Mouth never let her go anywhere, so it would mean a lot to her."

Shadow considered this for a moment before responding. "How about this? We arrange a day for you to take her there. I'll have Vampire and King stationed outside the bookstore, keeping watch. You can take my truck—it's got blacked-out windows. Mouth won't be looking for my vehicle. Tildie won't even know the brothers are there, so you can focus on her, knowing she's safe."

Relief and gratitude washed over me. "That would be perfect. I appreciate this, Shadow. How about next Monday, ten in the morning? By then, she should be walking without her crutches and able to enjoy herself fully."

Shadow nodded, standing as he stretched his back. "I'll talk to Vampire and King and confirm with you. It's a good plan. Now, I need to get my girls home. Mary still needs rest, though she'll fight me on it." He chuckled softly, walking over to Mary. He took the baby into his arms, then reached for Mary's hand, leading them toward the door.

I watched them leave, my thoughts already spinning with anticipation.

I couldn't wait to tell Tildie about the outing I had planned. But I'd wait until Shadow confirmed everything before saying a word.

I wouldn't take her out unless I knew she was fully guarded.

Mouth would never get his filthy hands on Tildie again. Not while I was breathing.

Marilyn was such a beautiful baby. Holding her in my arms felt like a dream. Mary was so kind to let me hold her for a while, and it stirred something deep within me—a longing I had kept buried for years.

I dream of having a child someday.

Being deaf might make it difficult, but with someone like Travis by my side, I feel like it could work.

Thank God Mouth never wanted children. He made sure I stayed up to date on my birth control shot, likely more for his convenience than anything else.

Summer came and sat down beside me, her warm presence grounding me. Mary started chatting with her, their conversation comforting even if I couldn't hear it. I let my gaze wander around the room, landing on Travis. He was deep in conversation with Shadow, his expression focused and serious.

Then, my eyes found the brunette who had approached him before. She was sitting with a blonde woman, both of them casting glances toward Travis and Shadow.

Old habits die hard.

Over the years, I've learned to "overhear" conversations by reading lips, and I couldn't help myself now.

The women were talking about Shadow. They couldn't understand why he would want to be with Mary. One of them called her a "Mary Sue," saying she was probably boring in bed.

Then the brunette shifted her focus to Travis.

"He's so hot," she said, her lips curving into a sly smile. "But until the deaf chick leaves, there's no point. She's taking all his time."

The blonde nodded, and their conversation drifted to Stonewall and why he'd been acting strange lately.

I felt someone approach the table and quickly looked away, not wanting to be caught watching.

It was Shadow, here to take Mary and the baby home. Shadow was always kind to me, but his presence didn't carry the same warmth as Travis's. He cuddled the baby close before taking Mary's hand to help her up. Mary turned to me with a soft smile to say goodbye before they left.

The men here take such good care of their women.

I want that.

I'm becoming more attached to Travis every day. I know I need to talk to him soon—stop being such a coward and tell him how I feel.

Summer touched my hand, pulling me from my thoughts. She was leaving, her kind smile telling me she goodbye even though I wasn't great company at the moment. My mind was too preoccupied.

I just want so much to stay here. To stay with Travis.

This club is so different from the Fire Dragons. Growing up in that clubhouse, there was no escaping the horrible things that happened. But here... here was different.

Even when the parties got wild, it was contained outside. Inside felt more like a bar—a place to unwind with music, dancing, pool games, and laughter. Sure, some of the men and women made out, but it never crossed the line into something too over the top.

The women here were cared for. Respected.

The men here were miles better than any I had ever known.

A pair of jean-clad legs appeared in front of me, pulling me from my thoughts. I didn't have to look up to know who it was.

Travis.

God, he was handsome. Especially when he gave me that crooked smile—the one I knew he reserved just for me.

"Ready for your leg massage?" he asked, holding out his hand for me to take.

"Yes, I'm ready," I signed, slipping my hand into his.

Travis had been giving me leg massages to help with my recovery, as Doc recommended. The first time, I'd been so uncomfortable I could barely sit still. Travis had noticed right away and offered to have Summer take over, but I'd refused.

I forced myself to relax after that, though a part of me still struggled. I liked his touch too much, and it made me feel... ashamed. That old voice in my head whispered that I was dirty, that I didn't deserve to feel something so good.

Travis helped me to my feet, balancing me on my crutches before stepping close to my side as we walked to my room.

When I stumbled over a step, his arms were around me instantly, holding me steady. His eyes met mine, filled with quiet reassurance.

He would never let me fall. Never let me be hurt.

And in that moment, I realized just how much Travis Baylor meant to me.

I love him.

And that terrifies me.

I love you, Matilda Westcott.

The thought filled my mind as I watched her settle on the bed, preparing for her leg massage. One day, I'd say those words to her. But not yet—not until we were both on the same page.

One day at a time, Travis. One day at a time.

Today, Tildie was wearing pink shorts and a silky floral shirt. She looked radiant, the soft colors complementing her delicate features. I couldn't help but smile, knowing she felt good in the clothes.

When I read her journal, I learned that Mouth had dressed her in ugly, baggy clothes out of jealousy, stripping her of even the smallest joys. She had written about how she wished she could wear pretty things like Brooke and the other women.

I wanted to change that for her.

That's why I'd asked Nikki and Mary to shop for everything Tildie would need, handing them my debit card along with her sizes, which I had carefully noted from the clothes she'd been wearing when we found her.

The club would have gladly covered the cost, but I needed this to come from me. A selfish part of me wanted to be the one to provide for Tildie, to give her whatever her heart desired.

"Are you ready?" I asked, rubbing my hands together to warm them up.

Tildie's wide, signature smile lit up her face. "Have at it," she said, her voice soft but playful.

I sat on the edge of the bed, gently taking her foot in my hands. Her feet were so small and dainty—delicate in a way that fascinated me.

I had never been a man with particular preferences when it came to women. To me, nothing else mattered as long as there was attraction and a genuine connection. But fuck, her feet turned me on. I feel weird even thinking about it, but it's true. I never thought feet could be sexual, but as I'm massaging Tildie's, all sorts of filthy thoughts are going through my head.

Right down to my cock.

Chill Travis. She's not even close to being ready.

I moved up to her calf, working the muscle carefully. As my hands moved, I glanced at Tildie and caught her watching me, her eyes fixed on the movements of my hands.

She was feeling something—curiosity, maybe even desire—but I could tell she didn't quite know how to process it.

"Does it feel good, Tildie?" I asked, pausing for a moment, hoping she'd open up about what she was feeling.

Her cheeks flushed a deep pink, and she bit her lip nervously before answering. "Yes, it feels nice. You have magic hands." She signed playfully, adding the gesture for giggling.

It was a first.

I'd never seen Tildie so playful, so at ease. It made my heart swell, and I couldn't stop myself from smiling back.

"I didn't think you could get any prettier, Tildie, but I was wrong," I said, winking at her. "I like seeing you happy and playful. It looks good on you."

She sighed softly, probably unaware that I could hear her. Tildie made sounds all the time, though she didn't realize it. I was sure with the help of a speech therapist, she could learn to speak if she wanted. Doc had mentioned looking into specialists, and I knew he'd follow through soon.

As I continued up her leg, I worked my hands gently around her knee and moved up to her thigh. I felt her shiver under my touch. She was enjoying this, trusting me a little more with each session.

But I wouldn't push her.

Not until she was ready to tell me everything.

Until she understood that I accepted her completely—exactly as she was—and that nothing could change how I felt about her.

I'd been reading everything I could about how to handle situations like hers, wanting to make sure I got it right.

Because Tildie wasn't just anyone. She was too important to me.

And I wasn't going to lose her.

10

I'm losing more of my shit with each day I don't have Tildie. Thoughts of that young fucker touching and holding my sweet girl fill my mind every fucking second of the day and night. I can't sleep and have been doing way too much coke to keep going, but I can't fall asleep and miss my chance to grab Tildie.

I just got back to the clubhouse after watching the roads for any sign of Tildie. It's almost midnight, and I know that she won't be leaving. I'll take a break and head back in the morning.

I look around the bar we are currently using as a clubhouse. I'm looking for Cross and spot him on a couch with a bitch bouncing on his dick. I grabbed a beer, swallowing some ecstasy, and went to sit beside him.

The blonde bitch on his lap licked her lips at me, leaning over to unbutton my pants, still riding Cross like a bull. Cross had his head laid back and eyes closed. He was so high he didn't know what was happening around him.

Finally, the ecstasy started to hit me. I stood, taking my cock out. "Turn around and face me," I grunted at the whore. She turned on Cross's lap, not missing a beat, bringing her face to eye level with my cock. "Suck me off while you fuck Cross," I commanded her.

I closed my eyes, imagining Tildie's blue gaze looking up at me, remembering how tiny her mouth looked wrapped around my cock, her beautiful tears sliding down her face as I fucked her mouth. I know if she could talk, she'd tell me how much she enjoyed it when I snuggled her close afterward.

With thoughts of Tildie, I was finally able to come, but without Tildie here, it wasn't the same. I pushed the bitch away, zipping my pants and sitting down, waiting for Cross to finish so I could talk to him, not that he was coherent enough to understand shit.

"Still no Tildie?" Flex asked, sitting down.

Flex wasn't much younger than me and a mean son of a bitch at forty-three. I know Brooke hated him. That made it all the sweeter when he claimed her after calling in a favor from her old man. I encouraged Flex to pursue Brooke. I hated the bitch and wanted her gone. Brooke made things hard for me by sleeping in the same bed as Tildie when she found out I was going to see my sweet girl.

"Not yet. Has she contacted Brooke?"

"Not that I know of. I asked her like you wanted. Even slapped her around a little bit, and threatened the kid to make sure she wasn't fucking lying to me," Flex said, pulling the blonde bitch on his lap for his turn.

"Shadow will fucking pay for taking my sister and killing my dad," Cross mumbled, opening his eyes to a slit so fucked up he couldn't move. Cross was such a fucking waste.

"Flex, take the bitch somewhere else," I growled. Not wanting to talk in front of the whore. We should have Church, but Cross is incompetent, and a lot of brothers are going to vote him out, including me. Once Flex moved, I looked at Cross. "Have you got any new information?"

"No, our hacker can't break through. We may have just to shoot the place to hell," Cross slurred, his voice fading as he passed out.

"You stupid motherfucker," I snarled. "I'll kill you myself if I lose Tildie." I got up, spitting on Cross, not giving a fuck who saw. Dumb bastard was worthless. I was going to take matters into my own hands.

I need my sweet Matilda back before I go crazy.

11

It felt amazing to have full use of my leg again.

For the last few days, I'd been putting more and more weight on it, and now I was walking normally. I was still cautious, but so far, so good.

Today, Travis and I were walking outside together. We were taking the path that led to Shadow's house—a tree-lined trail that offered welcome shade on this hot summer day.

In just a week, Travis would return to work, and the thought already left me feeling a sense of loss. For the past two months, he had been my constant companion, my anchor. I didn't know what I'd do without him by my side every day.

And then there was the question of what came next for me. Now that I was healed, I wasn't sure where I'd go or what I'd do.

But I wasn't stupid—I knew Travis wanted more than friendship. He wanted a relationship.

And I wanted that too.

But first, he needed to know the truth about me.

He deserved that.

A gentle squeeze of my hand pulled me from my thoughts. I looked up to see Travis watching me, his brown eyes filled with curiosity.

"What are you thinking, Tildie?" he asked, his voice steady but soft.

I took a deep breath, my heart pounding. *Just say it, Tildie,* I chastised myself.

"Travis," I signed, my hands trembling, "I really like you, but there are things you don't know about me, and I need to tell you... things that may change how you see me." Tears filled my eyes, blurring my vision.

Travis stepped closer, cupping my face in his hands and forcing me to look at him. "Tildie, there is nothing you can tell me that would change how I feel about you. Nothing. Do you understand?"

Even without hearing his tone, I knew the words were forceful, his expression resolute. His soft brown eyes never left mine as his thumbs brushed away my tears.

"I want to believe that," I signed, tears streaming down my cheeks. "I really do. But Mouth did things to me... things that make me dirty and broken. You deserve better than a broken, deaf girl."

The words spilled from me in a flood. I had never spoken about what Mouth had done to anyone but Brooke, and now the weight of those memories threatened to crush me.

"You're wrong, Tildie," Travis said, his voice firm yet gentle. "I'm lucky to have you. I don't care what happened with Mouth—whatever it is, we'll work through it together. The past is the past. As far as I'm concerned, our lives started the moment fate put us in each other's path. And I don't ever want to hear you call yourself broken or dirty again. Got me?"

I nodded, unable to speak as fresh tears spilled over. Travis pulled me into his arms, holding me tightly and rocking me gently until my sobs subsided.

When I finally pulled back, I looked up into his concerned face. "I'm scared, Travis," I signed. "I want so much to believe it won't matter, but what if you change your mind when you hear everything?"

Travis smiled softly, his hands resting on my shoulders as he leaned down to meet my gaze. "Tildie, there's not a single thing you could tell me that would change how I see you. Your smile brightens my day, your presence gives me peace, and you are so beautiful inside and out. I can't picture my life without you in it. Believe me when I say nothing will ever change that. Don't be scared. Let that feeling go, and let's enjoy what we have. When you're ready, we'll talk about what happened with Mouth. But it won't change how I feel about you, so never be afraid to tell me anything. I'm here for you."

"How did I get so lucky to find you?" I signed, blinking back fresh tears. "I used to think God was ignoring me... but then I woke up to you."

Travis hugged me again, his arms warm and steady around me.

"Enough serious talk for today," he said with a grin as he pulled back. "Let's enjoy the fact that today I get to take you on the back of my bike for a ride."

I clapped my hands, excitement bubbling up as he took my hand, and we started walking back toward the clubhouse.

Shadow had spoken to us yesterday, saying he thought it would be safe for me to join the club ride as long as Travis and I wore helmets to avoid being easily recognized. With over thirty members going, he was confident I'd be protected.

I couldn't wait.

I'd been on the back of a bike plenty of times with Mouth, but this time would be different. With Travis, everything was different.

I love him.

He's becoming the center of my world, and as we walked hand in hand, I resisted the urge to pinch myself.

This was everything I had ever dreamed of—and it was real.

I can't wait for Mouth to get what he deserves for all the hurt he has caused Tildie. I know Mouth treated her roughly during the sex he forced on her. Doc said she had vaginal tearing when they examined Tildie. Doc only let me know so I could better help her work through everything that happened to her.

I'd been researching therapists who specialize in working with the hearing impaired. I wanted Tildie to have the option to talk with someone who could help her process everything she'd been through. I knew there were things she'd never feel comfortable sharing with me, no matter how close we were.

While Tildie went inside to change for the ride, I pushed my bike out of the garage. My bike was my baby.

A blue Harley Davidson Fat Boy.

I'd saved for years to buy it outright, and it was worth every penny. I'd kept it in pristine condition, and until now, I'd never had a passenger. Tildie would be the first.

Straddling the bike, I rolled over to where the other brothers were gathering. Today marked the first Sunday joy ride for several of them in a while. Mary's dad had arrived yesterday, bringing his girlfriend, and they were watching over Marilyn and Preston. Rowena was at her grandparents', so Lord and Sophia were here too.

I hadn't been on a Sunday ride since Tildie was hurt. Leaving her alone, even for an afternoon, hadn't been an option.

Viking walked over, his usual cool expression in place. "I know you usually ride toward the back, but Moreno's switching with you today so you can ride in the middle. I know you already know this, but don't leave the group for any reason. That fucker's still out there, so be safe." He paused, his eyes narrowing slightly. "You got your gun, right?"

"Yeah, I'm armed," I replied, patting my cut where the gun was holstered.

Being one of the youngest members of the club could be frustrating sometimes—older members like Viking occasionally treated me like I didn't know what I was doing. But I knew it came from a good place. They just wanted to look out for me.

Viking nodded and walked away, heading to his bike at the front of the formation. He'd been great about letting me take leave from *The Unlimited* while I looked after Tildie. Hell, he'd even made sure I kept getting paid. My bank account balance had been steadily growing, even though I hadn't worked in two months.

I went back on Tuesday. Tildie was well enough to be on her own now.

My thoughts scattered as I saw her coming out of the clubhouse.

Damn, she looked good.

She wore fitted leathers, a blue top that showed just enough of the curve of her breasts, and black boots that made her legs look longer. The outfit hugged her curves in all the right places. She was stunning —so much so that it stopped me in my tracks.

The only thing that would make her more beautiful was my property patch on her back. And she'd have it—sooner rather than later, if I had anything to say about it.

I grinned as she walked toward me, smiling brightly. She was happy, and that was everything I wanted for her.

"Hop on, sexy," I signed when she reached me, flashing her a teasing smile.

Tildie lowered her lashes, a soft blush coloring her cheeks as she gave me a sweet smile. She climbed on behind me with practiced ease, and I handed her a helmet. Because of her glasses, the helmet didn't cover her face entirely, but I wasn't worried. Mouth wouldn't get near her today.

After securing my own helmet, I glided into formation beside King and Lettie.

Tildie placed her hands on my waist, holding on lightly. I knew she was experienced riding on the back of a motorcycle, but I wanted her closer. I needed to feel her against me.

Reaching down, I took her hand and guided it around my waist, repeating with the other hand until she understood. She scooted forward until her chest pressed against my back.

Right where I wanted her.

Shadow raised his arm, signaling for the ride to begin, and we roared out of the gate.

I loved these Sunday joy runs. There was no pressure, no tension like there was on club runs where we had to stay sharp for the illegal shit we were doing.

This was different.

Just the open road, the wind in my face, the beauty of the scenery, the brotherhood of my club...

And now, Tildie at my back.

Peace.

12

The ride felt like an adventure—my first real one. The breathtaking scenery and the wind brushing against my face made me feel free in a way I'd never experienced before.

When Mouth took me out, it was always at night, straight to wherever the club was hiding. No scenic detours, no stops to take in the world. My childhood was even more confining. There were no vacations, no day trips. The clubhouse was our home, and the club women were our mother figures, teachers, and everything in between.

Mouth had insisted on keeping me hidden. He claimed it was to protect me, to keep me safe because I was fragile and the world was dangerous.

But I knew the truth.

Mouth was delusional. And in his twisted obsession, he violated me in countless ways.

A gentle touch on my leg brought me back to the present. I looked down at Travis's hand, his thumb brushing softly against me, grounding me. Up ahead, the line of bikes slowed, signaling we were about to stop.

I couldn't help but notice how different this ride was from what I'd grown up with. Here, ol' ladies were welcomed on rides. They were part of the experience, riding proudly behind their men. With the Fire Dragons, it was unheard of. Ol' ladies stayed home to look after babies, while club women were the ones who joined the men on the road.

These men were a different breed entirely.

We pulled into a bar called *Ironstone*, the bikes parking in neat, precise rows. Travis stopped the bike, and I climbed off, stretching to ease the stiffness in my legs.

"Does your leg feel okay?" he asked, concerned, his eyes searched mine.

"Yes, just the usual stiffness from riding. I'm good," I assured him with a smile.

He twined his fingers through mine, leading me toward the bar and then to the bathrooms. "We'll meet back out here," he signed before waiting for me to step into the women's restroom.

Being in a public place was new to me, and I couldn't deny the intimidation that came with it. I felt a light touch on my arm and turned to see Nikki smiling at me.

"Are you enjoying the ride, Tildie?" she asked.

Before I could respond, Lettie's face appeared in front of me, her grin teasing. "Of course she's enjoying the ride—holding on to that hunk of a man? How could she not?"

Nikki rolled her eyes, swatting Lettie on the head playfully. "Ignore her," she said, laughing. "Are you?"

I nodded, pulling a small notepad and pencil from my pocket. *Yes, very much so,* I wrote before showing it to her.

"I'm glad, Tildie," Nikki said, her smile soft and kind.

After finishing up, we washed our hands and stepped back into the bar, where Travis and Vampire were waiting. Vampire was intimidating, as always, despite the small smiles he reserved for me. I couldn't imagine being in a relationship with him like Nikki was. I much preferred Travis's calming presence, his quiet steadiness.

"Let's get a drink before we have to head back," Travis said, his hand resting protectively on the small of my back as we followed Nikki and Vampire to a table.

The *Ironstone* was a clean bar with outdoor seating and live music. The atmosphere was lively, with bikers and locals mingling throughout. It lacked the rough edge I'd grown used to in Fire Dragons bars, where tension simmered in the air, waiting to boil over.

Travis handed me a drink menu, his lips twitching with amusement. "Sorry, party girl, only non-alcoholic for you."

I signed *Boo* with a thumbs-down, playing along. Truthfully, I wasn't interested in alcohol. Growing up, drinking never led to anything good. Mouth had been especially cruel when he was drunk, and my father had been no different.

"What'll it be?" Travis asked, his teasing smile still in place.

"Just a Coke," I replied, though I couldn't shake the sudden unease creeping in. Signing in public was making me feel self-conscious, like I was putting myself on display. My gaze darted around the room, catching the glance of a pretty blonde waitress. The way she looked at me wasn't kind as she walked to our table and spoke to Vampire.

Vampire stood abruptly, his expression dark. Something was happening, but I didn't know what. The waitress wasn't facing me, so I didn't know what she said.

Travis touched my face gently, drawing my attention back to him. "I have some good news for you," he said.

"I like good news," I replied, trying to focus on him instead of the tension building around us.

"I've arranged for a trip to the bookstore tomorrow morning," he said, a grin breaking across his face.

"Really? Tomorrow?" Excitement shot up inside me.

"Yep. We'll leave around ten."

"A real bookstore! I can't wait." The words slipped out before I could stop them, and I threw my arms around him, hugging him in my excitement.

Both of us froze for a moment, surprised by my boldness. My cheeks burned as I quickly pulled back, and signed, "Thank you."

Travis chuckled, his expression thoughtful as he watched me. I lowered my eyes, sipping my Coke to hide my embarrassment.

But I couldn't stop the excitement coursing through me.

A bookstore.

It felt like Christmas Eve, waiting impatiently for the morning to come.

I hadn't planned to tell Tildie about the bookstore trip until we were alone, but that waitress forced my hand.

She had the audacity to look at Vampire and ask if Tildie was "retarded" and whether she'd need a bib.

What the actual fuck?

Who says something like that—especially right in front of her?

Thank God Tildie didn't catch it. She hadn't been looking directly at the waitress when it was said, but I knew she felt the shift in energy. She knew something had happened, and it bothered her.

Vampire, however, caught every word, and from the dark look on his face, that waitress was about to learn a very hard lesson. My mom raised me to respect women, to never lift a hand against one, but at that moment, I felt my hand flex involuntarily. The thought of how

Tildie would've felt if she'd known what was said made my blood run hot.

No one was allowed to hurt Tildie again—man or woman—without answering for it.

I watched her as she sat quietly, pretending to focus on her Coke.

When I told her about the bookstore trip, the excitement that lit up her face was everything. Her hug—spontaneous and unprompted—was a huge step for us. It wasn't just the hug itself; it was what it represented.

Tildie trusted me.

That one hug meant the world. I only wished it could've happened in private, but I wasn't going to dwell on that. She had initiated the contact, and that was all that mattered.

I finished my beer and leaned back in my seat, letting the noise of the bar fade into the background. I never drank much, especially when riding, and the night my mom died had killed any fascination with it. The man who beat my mom to death had been drunk and high on coke, and when I finally killed him, I don't think he even felt it.

A nudge to my shoulder brought me back to the present.

"Time to head back," Vampire said, standing and offering Nikki his hand.

I glanced at Tildie, who was already up, watching me expectantly. I took her hand, leading her through the bar and out the front door.

Finally—quiet.

How people spent hours in that kind of noise was beyond me. It just wasn't for me.

Outside, I let go of Tildie's hand and handed her the helmet. "Time to get back on the road, beautiful," I signed, stealing a quick kiss before straddling my bike and putting on my helmet.

A moment later, I felt Tildie climb on behind me. This time, without any coaxing, she wrapped her arms around my waist, pressing her front against my back.

Exactly where I wanted her.

I revved my bike, waited for my turn, and pulled into formation, heading back down the mountain. The wind, the open road, and the rhythm of the ride brought a sense of calm I desperately needed.

But that calm was short-lived.

As we neared the clubhouse, a chill crept down my spine, and the hair on my arms stood on end.

We were being watched.

My eyes scanned the surroundings, searching for any sign of movement, but I didn't see anything. The feeling didn't leave, though. It lingered, prickling at my senses until we finally rode through the gates and were safely back inside.

Mouth.

There was no doubt in my mind he was out there. Watching. Angry.

And waiting for his moment.

Once we parked, I walked Tildie inside, staying close until she was settled. Only then did I return to the garage to put my bike away.

But I couldn't let it rest.

I needed to talk to Vampire about security for tomorrow's trip. We couldn't afford to let our guard down, not even for a second.

Tildie was too important to me.

And I wasn't taking any chances.

Climbing into the tree, I got comfortable pulling out my binoculars. I was fucking late getting here today. Cross had me doing shit for the Fire Dragons.

I could still see the front of the clubhouse from my position in this tree. I had to walk a mile to get here without being seen. The Devil's House had men walking the outside grounds, so I had to be careful. Once I was in the tree, they never knew I was there.

I knew Tildie now had her cast off, and the little fucker Reader was going back to work on Tuesday. I sent one of the club sluts into the bar he works at to find out what she could. Julie told the bartender she was an old friend and found out Reader would be back on Tuesday evening.

I heard the rumble of motorcycles and knew they must be coming back from the usual Sunday run. So I put the binoculars to my face and watched as they rode by where I was in the tree.

A loud growl burst from my chest as I spotted my little girl on the back of that son of a bitch's bike.

I let out another angry growl when I saw her holding onto him, dressed like a club slut. Fucking hell no! My sweet Tildie was showing her tits! I could see them bouncing over the top of the tank she was wearing.

I pointed my gun, wanting to shoot that cocksucker right in the head, but my pistol didn't have the range, and I couldn't guarantee I wouldn't hit Tildie. So I couldn't take the chance. Besides, the little prick would return to work on Tuesday, and I would get my chance.

I needed to get her away from them. These men were corrupting her, making her do things I know she can't be comfortable doing. Like dressing like a two-bit whore. Tildie's body is for my eyes only. No other man gets to see what lies beneath her clothes. Her fucking body belongs to me. I made Tildie a woman and taught her how to pleasure a man.

I can still remember the first time I fucked Tildie. She had just turned sixteen and was so beautiful. She was scared at first; me being so much bigger, but after a bit, she got into it, and I had never felt what I did when I was inside my sweetie. We have a connection that cannot be broken.

I climbed out of the tree. There was no point staying here right now. Tildie wouldn't be leaving again today. And I need to relieve the anger I'm feeling right now. It's consuming me, and someone will feel my fist before the day ends. I can't go much longer like this. I need her back.

13

I had just dozed off when I heard her. Tildie was thrashing around in the bed, sobbing in her sleep.

Another nightmare.

I pushed myself off the cot, climbed onto the bed, and carefully pulled her to me. I rocked her, holding her still until she slowly woke up and came back to the present. This has become an almost nightly thing. I hate that Tildie suffered through these nightmares alone before I started sleeping in her room.

Tildie clung to me as she calmed down, her arms wrapped around my waist, her small hands fisted into my back. I rubbed small circles on her back as I held her close. I found that helped to calm her faster.

I felt her breathing even out and knew she was back with me one hundred percent. I felt her lips touch my chest, causing me to inhale a breath. I slowly let it out as I felt her kiss my chest again and felt her hands caressing my back.

What was Tildie doing?

Not that I'm complaining, but I never expected her to do this.

I pulled back to look into her face. Tildie brought her hand up and signed, "Kiss me."

My eyes widened in surprise. "Are you sure that's what you want?"

"It's what I need. To forget," she signed, her eyes pleading.

I lowered my head, taking her lips in a soft kiss, keeping the kiss slow for a few minutes before licking her lips, working my tongue inside her mouth, and urging her tongue to play with mine. It wasn't long before Tildie kissed me with a passion I didn't know if she was ready for right now.

Her hands were moving up and down my back. The way she was touching me was making it hard for me to keep my hands from roaming her curvy little body. And when she was started to rub on me—fuck, I wanted her.

My cock was hard, and I knew she had to feel it as she moved against me. My hand moved up her side, my thumb stroking the side of her breast over her nightgown, causing a sweet little moan from Tildie.

I kissed my way down her neck, taking cues from her about how far she wanted to go. My hand closed over her breast as my mouth moved back up to take her lips. I played with her breast for a few minutes before sliding my hand down to cup one plump ass cheek. My other hand stayed threaded through her hair, guiding the kiss.

I wanted to get completely lost in Tildie right now, but knew I couldn't. So I had to go slow and stay aware of signs when it became too much.

I kneaded her butt cheek before pulling her closer to my hard cock. And that's when I felt it. Her body stiffened slightly. I moved my hand back up to her back, but continued kissing her for another minute before pulling away and looking down at her. Her blue eyes shone with her arousal. Her face was soft and beautiful.

Tildie moved back, putting some space between us. "You didn't have to stop," she signed, looking guilty.

"It's fine, Tildie. I enjoyed what we did, and I don't mind going slow," I assured her, stroking her cheek.

"But, Mouth always said that it hurt a man to stop," she said, her cheeks turning pink.

Fucking Mouth.

"Tildie, it doesn't hurt a man to stop. It's hard sometimes to pull back, but trust me, a real man can do it. The feeling can be uncomfortable, but we'll survive. Trust me, okay?"

"I just feel like it's unfair for you to have someone like me. I don't know if I work right." I saw tears form in her eyes.

I took her face in my hands. "Tildie, did you enjoy what we just did?" I asked, watching her closely.

Blushing hard, she answered, "Yes, it felt good. Nothing like what I expected."

"Then trust me, you work just fine. There's no rush to do everything at once. We'll go slow, and when it happens, it happens. How about you let me hold you for the rest of the night while we sleep? Just hold each other. Would you like that?"

"Yes, I would like that."

"You have a big day tomorrow, so let's get some sleep."

I pulled her to me and arranged her so she would be comfortable, stroking her back while her head lay on my chest. I didn't lie when I said it would be uncomfortable to stop because, right now, I want nothing more than to rub one out for relief. But I can't leave Tildie right now while she's vulnerable. My dick will just have to calm down.

After an hour, I felt her fall asleep, and I followed, contently holding the woman I love in my arms.

14

Last night with Travis was amazing. I hadn't known intimacy with a man could feel so good, so freeing. Sex with Mouth hurt, and sometimes it would make me bleed, but he never seemed to notice or care. And kissing consisted of him shoving his tongue in my mouth until I wanted to gag. I felt sick just at the thought.

That's why I wanted Travis to kiss me—I needed to create different memories, memories that erased the ones tied to Mouth.

I just wanted to forget everything about that man.

But today was about moving forward. Today was a good day.

Travis was taking me to a bookstore. Most people might think it was silly, getting so excited about something so simple, but they hadn't grown up as I did. They hadn't spent their entire lives shut away, never experiencing the little joys most people take for granted.

Like going to a bookstore.

Travis had gotten up before me, already showered and dressed. He'd said he would wait for me in the kitchen, and we could have breakfast before we left. I showered quickly, picking out a cute yellow sundress with matching low-heeled sandals. Before Travis, I'd never cared much about how I looked. Part of me had always wanted to dress prettier, but another part wanted to avoid drawing attention to myself.

Now, though, I wanted to look pretty—for him.

I tied my hair into a ponytail and glanced at the makeup sitting in the bathroom. I didn't even know where to begin with it, so I left it alone. I hated my glasses, but I needed them. A girl had to see, after all.

When I entered the kitchen, I saw Travis sitting at the table with Fuse, Shay, baby Preston, and Silver. As soon as he saw me, he stood and motioned for me to sit beside him.

I shook my head, signing that I would get my food first.

I knew Travis would've insisted on getting it for me, but I needed to do some things for myself. His smile told me he understood, and he sat back down.

I made myself a plate of pancakes and grabbed a glass of orange juice. The food here was so different from what I'd grown up with. At the Fire Dragons' clubhouse, meals were an afterthought. After my dad died and the club fell apart, everyone fended for themselves. Mouth had kept a small refrigerator in his room, and whatever I ate came from there. He'd never officially claimed me, but it was understood—by everyone—that I was his responsibility.

Was.

I carried my plate to the table, and Travis immediately stood again, ever the gentleman. I smiled as I sat, noting the warm greetings from the others at the table.

"You look pretty today, Tildie. I like you in yellow," Travis signed, flashing me that crooked smile that always made my insides melt.

"Thank you," I signed back, focusing on my food to hide my blush.

One of the hardest things about being deaf is that if you're not actively engaged in a conversation, you miss everything. It can feel isolating, especially when you don't hear someone approaching, like when Doc sat down beside me. I jumped, startled.

"Sorry, didn't mean to scare you," Doc said, his face apologetic.

I pulled my notepad from my dress pocket and wrote: *It's okay.*

"Tildie, I'm working on getting you appointments with hearing specialists. Did you ever visit a doctor?" he asked, speaking slowly so I could read his lips.

I thought for a moment before writing: *No, never.*

"Was there a reason why?"

I sighed, writing: *Dad was paranoid. He believed the government controlled everything, including healthcare. The only care we ever got was from the club medic.*

Doc frowned slightly, a sadness softening his eyes. "What about your glasses?"

I hesitated before writing: *When Dad was gone on a long run, one of the club women noticed I couldn't see well. She took me to the Walmart eye doctor and got me glasses. She told Dad they weren't prescription, just ones she'd picked up in the store.*

I felt embarrassed admitting it, like my upbringing was something to be ashamed of.

Doc smiled warmly, patting my hand. "Tildie, don't be embarrassed. A lot of us didn't have ideal childhoods. What matters is that you're here now, and we'll make sure you get the care you need."

With that, he rose and left the table, leaving me with a strange mix of gratitude and vulnerability.

Travis touched my hand, drawing my attention. "He's right, Tildie. My own childhood had its problems too. One day, I'll tell you about it, but not today. Today is about you. So, finish up, and we'll be on our way."

His words, his steady gaze—they filled me with warmth. I smiled, giving him a thumbs-up before turning back to my breakfast.

I watched Tildie finish her breakfast, and I couldn't help but smile. Tildie always looks pretty, but yellow was definitely her color. The way it highlighted her features and brought out the warmth in her complexion—it was stunning.

Jesus, I thought, *I sound like a chick.* But it was true. She looked beautiful.

Fuse, Shay, and Silver had left the table earlier, giving Doc and Tildie some privacy. I was glad for it. Tildie gets embarrassed so easily over things she has no reason to be ashamed of.

When Tildie set her fork down, signaling she was done, we headed outside to Shadow's truck, parked behind the clubhouse. I opened the passenger door, quickly realizing she'd never be able to climb in on her own.

"I'll lift you," I signed, placing my hands around her waist and lifting her effortlessly into the seat. The feel of her beneath my hands was warm and comforting, a reminder of how much she meant to me.

Once she was settled, I closed the door, walked around to the driver's side, and got in.

"Are you ready, beautiful?" I asked, glancing at her with a grin.

She gave the sign for chuckling, then answered with a smirk. "What do you think?"

"My girl's got a sassy side. I like it," I teased, winking as I started the truck and pulled out onto the road.

As we drove, I kept one eye on Tildie, watching her take in the world around her. Her gaze flitted from the trees to the shops we passed, her expression filled with curiosity. It broke my heart to think of the way she grew up, confined to the Fire Dragons' clubhouse, hidden from the world.

After twenty minutes, I turned into the parking lot of *Discover a Tale,* a three-story bookstore that was heaven for any book lover.

Tildie's excitement was palpable. She unbuckled her seatbelt, waiting for me to come around and help her down.

I loved that about her—that she didn't let her past dull her joy or stop her from embracing new experiences. Not everyone could do that.

I scanned the area as I walked to her side of the truck, spotting Vampire sitting in a car across the street. King was likely stationed behind the building, and I knew Moreno was inside, blending in as a customer. The brothers were thorough, and I appreciated their protection.

Opening the door, I couldn't help but grin as Tildie practically jumped into my arms. I set her down gently on the pavement and gave her a teasing smile.

"I hope they're not closed," I said.

Tildie swatted my arm playfully. "Don't even joke like that."

I laced my fingers through hers, and together we walked inside.

The shop smelled of old books, leather, and history—a mix that instantly relaxed me. Tildie stopped just inside, taking it all in. Her expression was pure wonder as her eyes roamed over the winding staircases and rows upon rows of books.

"Welcome back, Reader," Randal, the owner, called out. His snowy white hair and mustache paired with his sharp blue eyes gave him a wise, grandfatherly appearance. "And who is this lovely young woman?"

I signed to Tildie, introducing her to Randal, and to my surprise, Randal began signing himself.

"Hi, I'm Randal," he said, his hands moving fluidly. "And you are?"

Tildie's face lit up. "I'm Tildie Westcott, and I am so excited to be here and explore all these books," she signed back, her joy evident.

"Well, Miss Tildie, it's a pleasure to have you here. Anything in particular you're looking for?"

"No, not really. I love all books, but I do have a soft spot for classic romance, like *Pride and Prejudice*," she replied.

"An excellent choice," Randal said with a smile. "The classics section is on the second floor, aisle two. Enjoy your exploration."

Tildie beamed at him, and I felt a surge of gratitude toward the old man for his kindness.

As she strolled deeper into the store, I spotted Moreno on the third floor, sitting in a chair with a book in his lap. He looked bored out of his mind. I stifled a laugh. A bookstore wasn't exactly Moreno's idea of fun, but he was doing his job.

"Go ahead and start looking around," I told Tildie. "If you see something you want, pick it up and put it on the counter. I'll take care of it when we're done."

Predictably, she protested. "It's okay. I don't need anything. I'll just enjoy looking."

I stepped closer, brushing a strand of hair from her face. "Tildie, listen to me. If you see something you want, I'm getting it for you. It makes me happy to do this for you, so don't make me follow you around buying everything you touch," I said with a wink.

"Okay," she relented, though she added, "I feel like I'm taking advantage of you."

"There's nothing I wouldn't do for you," I said, giving her a gentle nudge toward the shelves. "Now go enjoy this place."

I watched as she wandered through the aisles, her fingers grazing the spines of books as if savoring the feel of them. Her expression was a mix of awe and joy, and I knew this was a moment she'd remember forever.

And so would I.

15

This had been the most incredible three hours of my life—aside from meeting Travis, of course. At first, I tried to hide my excitement, worried it might make me look childish. I mean, how many nineteen-year-olds get giddy over books? But it didn't take long before I couldn't contain it anymore, and honestly, I stopped caring. This bookstore was amazing, and I loved every second of being here.

I had told myself I wouldn't buy anything. That resolve lasted about fifteen minutes. By the time we were done, I had ten books in my arms. Travis didn't even blink when we checked out.

As we walked out the front door, I waved goodbye to Randal, who had been so sweet. Knowing sign language had made it easy for me to talk with him, and it felt like I'd made a new friend.

"I come here every few weeks," Travis said as we stepped onto the sidewalk. "So we'll be back."

"It's such a wonderful place," I replied, letting him take my hand. "I can see why you come here all the time."

We walked down the street toward the truck, and as we did, I felt the unmistakable sensation of being watched. I stopped, glancing around, but saw nothing out of the ordinary. *It's just my imagination,* I told myself.

Travis lifted me into the truck, and that's when I saw him.

Mouth.

He was standing at the window of the store next door, his face twisted into that sick, familiar smile. My blood ran cold as his lips moved silently. *I'm coming for you, sweet girl.*

Then he was gone.

My body began to shake, the terror of seeing him overwhelming me. Memories surged forward, unwelcome and vivid, and I instinctively tried to retreat into myself, to shut everything out.

Travis's hand wrapped around mine, grounding me, but my panic made me want to pull away. The fear, the shame—it all came rushing back.

"Tildie," Travis's voice broke through my haze as he cupped my face, forcing me to look at him. His expression was calm but intense. "What did you see?"

I shook my head, not wanting to answer.

"Tell me," he pressed, his tone steady but firm. "Was it Mouth?"

Tears filled my eyes as I nodded, lifting a trembling hand to point at the window where I'd seen him.

Travis didn't hesitate. He grabbed his phone, typing something quickly before setting it aside. Then, his hands returned to my face, his thumbs brushing away my tears.

"Tildie," he said, his voice steady, "Mouth will never touch you again. I swear to you. You're safe with me. I need you to trust me, okay? We're going back to the clubhouse, and we'll talk more there." He brought my hands to his lips, his soft brown eyes locking with mine. "Do you trust me to keep you safe?"

I drew in a shaky breath, forcing myself to push the memories back into the dark corners of my mind where they belonged. Looking into Travis's eyes helped; they were warm, strong, and reassuring.

"I trust you, Travis," I whispered, managing a small, shaky smile.

He nodded, starting the truck and pulling into traffic.

I clasped my hands tightly in my lap, wishing I'd kept one of my new books in the front seat so I could escape into its pages. Why did Mouth have to ruin this day of all days?

Glancing at Travis, I found him smiling at me, his expression full of reassurance.

But no matter how much I wanted to stay calm, the fear lingered. *What if Mouth succeeds?*

The thought was paralyzing. I knew how dangerous he was, how relentless. And now that I'd found Travis, the idea of losing him—of being dragged back into Mouth's control—was unbearable.

What if he kills Travis?

I watched him kill a man one night who thought I was a club girl and grabbed me, pinning me against a wall. Mouth caught him and pushed the man to his knees, and then shot him in the back of the head.

On the highway, I noticed two motorcycles with *The Devil's House MC* cuts trailing us. A few minutes later, two more pulled in front of us. They were escorting us, keeping us safe.

These men really care about me. It was still hard to believe sometimes, coming from a club where women were treated as disposable. Here, even the club girls were treated well, and the old ladies were cherished.

I leaned back, trying to relax, and let out a breath of relief when we finally passed through the gates of the clubhouse. This place had become my sanctuary, the one place where I felt truly safe.

Travis parked the truck, came around to my side, and helped me down.

"Are you okay?" he asked, his eyes searching mine.

"Yes," I said softly. "Now that we're back here."

He grabbed the bag of books from the backseat and rested his hand on the small of my back as he guided me inside. The warmth of his touch, the steady presence of him, was a comfort I hadn't known I needed.

But as we walked through the clubhouse doors, a thought struck me—a strong, urgent desire. *I need to know Travis in every way.*

Physically. Emotionally.

I wanted to let go of my fear, to let Travis help me rewrite the memories that haunted me. I loved him, and I knew he cared deeply for me.

Tonight, I would talk to him. Tonight, I would take that step forward. Because Travis wasn't just the man who made me feel safe— he was the man I wanted to be with, fully and completely.

And I wouldn't let fear hold me back any longer.

Mouth had to be killed. It was only a matter of time before he made a move on Tildie or killed me. I couldn't keep sitting back, waiting for him to strike. We needed a plan—a trap to end this once and for all.

First, I needed to make sure Tildie was okay. Then, I'd go to Shadow. Tildie deserved a normal life, free from the shadow of that asshole lurking around every corner.

I walked Tildie to her room, placing her books on the side table. She looked calmer than she had earlier, her expression soft but thoughtful.

"I'm sorry Mouth ruined your day," I said, leaning against the doorframe. "I'd hoped he wouldn't find out you left the grounds."

Her hands moved confidently as she signed, "He didn't ruin my day; he only interrupted it. I can't tell you how much going to the bookstore meant to me. I know it probably sounds silly and maybe a little lame, but it was one of the best experiences of my life—one I'll remember forever."

A big smile lit up her face, and for the first time since we'd gotten back, it reached her eyes, showing she truly meant it.

"There's nothing silly about how you feel," I assured her, stepping closer. "I still get excited going to bookstores, and I've been to more of them than I can count. We're book lovers; it's just who we are. I'm glad that idiot didn't ruin it for you. I wanted it to be special."

I pulled her into my arms, holding her close for a moment before pulling back. "I need to talk to Shadow, but I'll come by in a few hours, and we'll have dinner together, okay?"

"Okay," she replied, already reaching for one of her books. "I was planning to read for a few hours anyway, so that works."

Our future house would definitely need a library with how much we both loved books. I gave her a quick kiss and headed down the hall.

As I turned the corner, my phone buzzed with a text. Shadow must have read my mind—he wanted me in his office.

I knocked on the door, and Viking opened it, stepping aside so I could enter. Inside, Shadow was seated at his desk, with Vampire, King, and Fuse gathered around. The only empty seat was beside Vampire, so I took it.

Shadow got straight to the point. "So, Tildie saw Mouth in a store window?"

"Yeah," I growled, the anger rising in my chest again. "It scared the shit out of her. I don't know how he knew she was at the bookstore."

"He's still watching the clubhouse somehow," Vampire said, his tone thoughtful. "We're completely surrounded by forest, so he could be anywhere. But something tells me he didn't see her leave—he probably just saw her by chance."

"Why do you say that?" Viking asked.

"Because King followed Reader and Tildie into town and didn't see any signs of Mouth or the Fire Dragons. I watched Reader walk her inside the bookstore. The store Mouth was in is a liquor store next door. My guess is he just happened to see her through the window when they were walking back to the truck," Vampire explained.

"That makes sense," Shadow agreed. "But it was still a close call. If he'd had enough time, he could've tried to take her."

"That's why we need to set a trap," I said firmly, my voice like steel. "I'm done waiting for that fucker to make a move. I want to take matters into my own hands."

"What the fuck are you thinking?" Shadow demanded, leaning forward, his eyes narrowing.

"I'll be the bait," I said, meeting his gaze head-on. "We implant a tracker in me, let him capture me, and let him take me back to wherever the Fire Dragons are hiding. That way, you could get Cross too."

The room went silent, the tension thick.

Finally, Viking broke it. "You know he'll kill you. After seeing you with Tildie, I'm sure he plans to."

"He won't," I replied confidently.

"What makes you so sure?" Shadow pressed.

"Because Mouth wants Tildie. If he hurts me, he knows she'll never come to him willingly. He'll use me as leverage for an exchange."

"You might be right," Fuse said, though his expression was grim. "But he can still mess you up while he waits."

"I have no doubt he'll beat the shit out of me," I admitted, "but I'm willing to take that risk. You'll have a trace on me, and you'll be able to move quickly."

Shadow leaned back in his chair, flipping a pen between his fingers as he thought. "So many things could go wrong. There's a real chance you could be seriously hurt or even killed. Are you sure about this?"

"I'm positive," I said, my voice steady. "We can't keep hiding our women and kids because we're scared of when they'll strike next. Especially now, with babies in the mix. We need to end this, and I trust you guys to get me out."

Shadow's eyes scanned the room, gauging the reactions of everyone present. Finally, he sighed, setting the pen down. "If you're one hundred percent sure, I'll have Doc here in the morning to implant the tracker. After that, we'll hold Church to iron out the details."

"I'm all in," I replied, standing. "See you in the morning."

As I walked out of the room, my thoughts were already on Tildie. There was a risk something could go wrong, but for her—for her peace and her future—I'd take that risk. She would never live in fear of Mouth again.

I couldn't believe what I saw as I walked past the window in the liquor store. My little Tildie is walking toward the parking lot hand in hand with that fucker Reader. She was smiling and looking like a beautiful little doll baby in that yellow dress and ponytail. My heart ached along with my body with the need for my special girl.

And pure rage.

I scanned the street and saw two other Devil's House assholes sitting on their bikes, watching as Reader lifted Tildie into the truck, his hand way too familiar with her. Fuck, they were guarding Tildie. I was outnumbered.

I watched as she got comfortable in her seat, and then when she looked up and caught my eyes, I saw her surprise and what looked like fear. I mouthed I was coming for her and hit the store exit.

I was right. They were turning her against me. I need to act quickly before they do too much damage to my and Tildie's relationship. We love each other, and once I have her back, I'll remind her of that.

I headed back to the bar the Fire Dragons were hiding out in. I sat drinking and coming up with a plan to get my girl back. I signaled Cross over to me. There was only one way to get Tildie back and get Cross on board.

This had to work, and I can't let Cross mess it up. Dumb fuck.

16

Travis was being extra attentive this evening. I feel like something is going on that I don't know about. Or maybe he just feels like me, that it's time to move forward in our relationship. I have a second chance, and I can't let my fears ruin that for me. I know it's not going to be easy to let go of my past, but with Travis, I feel like I can do anything.

I finished getting ready for bed, my nerves crazy. I had read hundreds of romance books, and you would think I would know how to approach Travis about sex, but I was a bundle of nerves. It wasn't like I didn't know what happened during sex. Bile rose in my throat as

I thought of all the ways Mouth had used me during what he called playtime.

I pushed those thoughts aside, focusing only on Travis and how he made me feel. That's why I wanted to have sex with Travis so that I could replace the awful memories of Mouth with the good ones I knew I would create with Travis. I know in my heart that he will never hurt me mentally or physically.

One of the club girls told me once that when you're in love, the sex is different, better. That it will feel different from a man who only wants sex and cares about himself. And Travis and I care about each other, so sex will be different. I just know it.

I trust him completely.

The door opened, and Travis walked in dressed in sweats and a t-shirt. I already felt myself turning red, even though I hadn't even asked him yet. I hope I didn't make a colossal fool of myself.

"Is something wrong, Tildie?" he asked, noticing me standing there staring at him like a twit.

"I don't know how to say this," I signed, getting ready to chicken out.

"Say what? You can tell me anything," Travis replied, looking puzzled and a little worried.

"I want to have sex with you." I worked my hands so fast I don't know if he understood, but I think he did by the shocked look on his face.

"What brought this on?"

I let out a breath I didn't even realize I was holding. "I feel like its time to move to the next step in our relationship. I want to make new memories to replace the horrible ones that live in my head. I need to do this, Travis."

Travis took my face in his hands, kissing me before saying, "Tildie, I want you to know that I love you, and there is nothing I want to do more than make love to you. But I need you to be sure it's what you want and not something you think I need. Do you understand what I'm saying?"

"I understand, and I want this. I need this. I love you too, and our being with each other helps replace bad images in my head with good ones. I've had so few good memories in my life I don't want to waste any more time making more of them."

He pulled me into his arms, holding me close before leaning back and kissing me softly. "Okay, Tildie, but if at any time you want to stop, I don't care how far we've gone, you let me know, and I'll stop. Please tell me you'll be honest and let me know. I won't get angry."

"I promise you," I replied as he backed away to get something out of the backpack.

I put my glasses on the nightstand, and took off my nightgown. I hadn't bothered to wear anything underneath, knowing what I was going to do. Travis turned around, surprise on his face at seeing me standing there naked. His brown eyes darkened with appreciation as they moved over me. I thought this would be hard for me, but I'm not afraid.

That club girl was right, and it will be different.

Shit, she was gorgeous. I wasn't expecting this. I figured I would hold Tildie while she slept tonight. I had no idea which way her mind was going. I needed to keep myself in check and go slow, make it good for her. Tildie didn't make it easy on me by getting naked right away; that surprised me. She must have really thought this through.

I took my t-shirt off and would leave my pants on for now. I had one hell of a hard-on and would wait until I got her ready before removing them. She had such a beautiful body, breasts that were more than a handful, with dusky nipples. A tiny waist with flared hips that grew into one hell of a curvy ass for someone so petite. And I like that she wasn't shaved bare around her pussy. I wasn't into that. I wanted a more natural look and those fucking tiny feet. I pictured those feet stroking my cock.

Stop Travis. This is about Tildie tonight. Pleasing her and making this feel good and special for her.

"Lay on the bed, Tildie," I said, watching as she did as I asked. I went to the side of the bed and lay next to her. "You're so beautiful; you give me pleasure simply looking at you," I praised her, going in for a kiss. I kept it soft until I felt her relax and then deepened it until she let my tongue inside to play with hers.

As we kissed, I allowed my hands to start moving over her breasts, playing with her nipples. I felt relief when I heard her sigh and thread her fingers through my hair, pulling me deeper into our kiss. I slowly moved my hand down her body and between her legs, making sure to keep the kiss going as a distraction. I took my finger and ran it between her pussy lips and groaned when I felt how wet she was, and I had to remind myself that even though she was enjoying this, I still had to go slow.

I broke the kiss, my lips moving down to her breasts and taking a luscious nipple in my mouth, biting it and sucking on it, then moving to the other nipple giving it the same attention while Tildie's hands roamed through my hair and down my back. I glanced up at her to see her eyes closed with pleasure.

God, it was harder than I thought to keep it slow, especially when she started moving against me. But I still needed to make sure she was ready. I continued kissing my way down to her stomach, pushing my body between her legs. She stiffened a little when she saw where I was headed.

I stopped and looked up at her to see her watching me; her face unsure. "Do you trust me, Tildie, to make you feel good and prepare you for more?"

She gave me a smile and a nod, laying her head back down on the pillow.

I kneeled between her legs, looking at the prettiest and only pussy I would ever see, glistening with her arousal. I needed a taste. I leaned down and gave a soft kiss on her mound, my fingers stroking her inner thigh while I blew softly on her pussy, waiting for her body to clue me to when she was ready for more.

When I heard her moan, I started to lightly lick and suck my way around her pussy. I was using my fingers to spread her open so I could suck on her clit. Then I inserted a finger inside her, playing with her, and was pleased when she started moving against me.

Fuck, she was so responsive.

And she thought she was broken. Tildie was driving me wild with her little moans. I was barely holding myself back. I could eat her pussy all night. But I needed to keep things moving. I could tell she was close to her orgasm. I inserted another finger into her pussy and used my tongue to work her clit. Tildie gave a loud moan I didn't think she was capable of when she came. I kept pleasuring her through her orgasm, enjoying her sweet juices.

I felt her body settle and moved off the bed to remove my sweatpants and roll on the condom I had gotten out of my bag earlier. I needed to be inside of Tildie. I got back on the bed where she lay watching me, a look of awe on her face. "Do you want to continue?" I asked her, praying she did. I would stop if she wanted no question, but I wanted her so much.

"I want to do everything, Travis," Tildie answered with a soft smile showing no fear that I could detect in her features.

I wasted no time laying beside her, pulling her body to mine and kissing her again. My mouth moving over her body until I felt her breathing increase and her body begin to fidget. I knew she was ready to take me. I lined my cock up with her pussy and entered her slowly. Fuck, she felt like heaven, the way her pussy gripped my cock.

I felt her stiffen and stopped to check on her. I looked into her beautiful face and asked, "Are you okay?"

"I'm fine. I want this," she signed, her fingers stroking my face.

I pushed my cock the rest of the way in and started to move, my strokes long and easy. Tildie started running her hands up and down my back, her fingers moving through my hair. I touched my lips to hers, coaxing her to deepen the kiss as I started thrusting faster in and out of Tildie. I reached down, my fingers playing with her clit, and groaned when she began to move against me because I couldn't hold on much longer.

Finally, I felt her pussy spasm around my cock and gave a few more quick thrusts. I growled with my release and couldn't believe how fucking good it felt. I kept my weight off Tildie with my elbows as I lay above her, my head buried in her neck, her hands stroking my back as I got my breathing under control.

I raised my head, looking into her eyes. "I love you, Tildie, and I'm never letting you go." Then, giving her a soft kiss before rolling to her side. I pulled the condom off, threw it in the trash can by the bed, and cuddled a sleepy Tildie into my side, running my fingers through her hair until her breathing evened as she fell asleep.

It was a long time before I fell asleep. My mind worried about what I had agreed to do. I hadn't changed my mind, but I prayed everything would go off without any problems. I wanted more than anything to start building a life with Tildie.

My beautiful little bookworm.

My soulmate.

17

I watched **Travis leave the kitchen to talk with Shadow**, and a soft smile spread across my face as I remembered last night. It was beyond anything I ever imagined. My romance books always painted love scenes as magical and perfect, but I thought they had to be exaggerated. Now I knew better.

When Travis told me to lie on the bed, my heart raced with anticipation and nerves. Part of me feared it would be like what

Mouth always did—quick, painful, emotionless, and something I had to endure rather than enjoy. But this...this was something entirely different.

And when I saw him fully naked. I almost backed out then, too. Travis wasn't as big as Mouth, but his cock was still intimidating, and I feared the pain I thought I would experience. But, I only experienced pleasure and found myself looking forward to next time.

Travis had been so patient, so gentle, guiding me through every moment. His touch was firm yet tender, his kisses slow and reverent. There were moments when panic clawed at me, memories threatening to pull me back into the past. I almost told him to stop, but each time, I reminded myself it was Travis. I ran my fingers through his thick, soft hair, grounding myself in the reality of being with someone who truly cared for me.

And afterward, the way he held me close, whispering that he loved me and wasn't letting me go, made my heart swell in a way I never thought possible. I still have so much healing to do—so many mental scars to work through—but with Travis by my side, I know I can face it all.

A soft touch on my arm pulled me from my thoughts, and I turned to see Shay sitting beside me, baby Preston in her arms. His chubby little hand gripped her shirt.

"I know that look you're wearing," Shay said with a sly smile. "You got lucky."

Her words hit me like a bolt of lightning, and I felt heat rush to my face. I knew my cheeks were probably as red as a tomato. How did she know? Did I look different? Was there some obvious sign I'd missed?

"I—" My hands faltered, and I quickly grabbed my notebook, scribbling, *How do you know?*

Shay's smirk widened as she glanced around the room, then leaned closer. "You've got that glow, girl. Trust me, it's unmistakable. And Reader? He's was walking like he's ten feet tall. I'd have to be blind not to put two and two together."

I buried my face in my hands, groaning silently, and Shay chuckled, clearly enjoying my embarrassment. She rested a hand on my shoulder, her expression softening. "Relax, Tildie. You don't have to tell me anything. It's enough that I know. He's a good guy, and you're lucky to have him."

I smiled and wrote quickly: *I know. I thank God for him every single day.*

Shay read the note and nodded, her eyes sparkling with approval. "Good. Hold on to that, because guys like Reader don't come around often."

I was about to respond when a shift in the air caught my attention. I glanced up to see Lexi, one of the club girls, watching me from across the room. Her expression was unreadable, but her gaze lingered a little too long for comfort.

Frowning, I turned back to Shay and scribbled: *Why is Lexi staring at me?*

Shay read the note, and a mischievous grin spread across her face. She leaned in conspiratorially. "I *might* have said you got lucky a little louder than I should have. What can I say? My voice carries."

I glanced back at Lexi, who was still watching me, her lips pursed as if deep in thought. Was she upset? Jealous? I didn't know how to feel about it.

Shay smirked, clearly unbothered. "Let her stare. She'll get over it."

I shifted uncomfortably. Back at the Fire Dragons' clubhouse, the club women were like family. They helped take care of us, looked out for us, and often acted as surrogate mothers. But here, the dynamic was different. There was an undercurrent of tension between the club women and the ol' ladies, something I didn't fully understand.

Still, I trusted Travis. He'd told me he hadn't been with any of the club girls, and I believed him. Lexi's stares didn't bother me—not really. I offered her a small smile, trying to ease whatever tension lingered, before turning back to Shay.

Shay handed me Preston, and I cradled him in my arms, marveling at his tiny features. He was so cute, his little hand wrapping around my finger, and my heart melted. Holding him filled me with a strange mix of joy and longing.

"Looks good on you," Shay said, nodding at the baby in my arms.

I gave her a sheepish smile. *Someday,* I wrote in my notebook.

Shay winked. "With Reader? I don't doubt it."

I blushed again, looking down at Preston as I gently rocked him. The thought of a future with Travis—a real future—was both exhilarating and terrifying. But for now, I focused on the present, waiting for Travis to return, knowing that with him by my side, anything was possible.

The tracker was in my arm, a small device that now held the power to either save me or lead me straight into danger. Kickstand monitored it from his laptop, his expression serious as he double-checked the signal's strength. Shadow had called an early meeting where we ran through every possible scenario and plan of action. We decided I would stick to a predictable routine—work and the clubhouse only. If the signal deviated from that routine, it would be the alarm that I'd been taken.

I won't lie. I was nervous as hell. Knowing the risks, the danger, and what was at stake didn't make this any easier. But for the first time since my mom died, I had something—someone—to lose.

And that someone was standing in the kitchen, holding Preston with such care and joy that it made my heart ache. Tildie was talking to Shay, her face lit up with one of her smiles that brightend my day. She looked so natural, so right, with a baby in her arms. The sight stirred something deep within me.

I wanted that—a family with Tildie.

I never thought about being a father before, but with Tildie, it didn't just seem possible; it seemed right. Sure, there would be challenges. Her deafness and everything she had endured in her life meant there would be a learning curve for both of us. But we could handle it. Together, we could handle anything.

I never knew my own father, and my mother didn't even know who he was. That didn't matter, though. I loved her, flaws and all. She did what she needed to survive, even if it eventually cost her life.

I pushed the thought aside as Tildie handed Preston back to Shay, giving the baby a gentle kiss on his chubby cheek. She turned toward me, her eyes lighting up when she saw me.

"Want to go for a walk before I head to work?" I asked, holding out my hand.

"I'd like that," she replied, slipping her smaller hand into mine. She turned to wave goodbye to Shay, who gave me a wink and a knowing smile. What was that about?

Tildie and I walked outside, hand in hand, the warm breeze carrying the scent of pine and wildflowers. The sun filtered through the canopy of trees, casting dappled light along the dirt path. The air was alive with the sound of chirping birds and the distant sound of the road.

I knew Mouth was out there somewhere, watching. He was always watching. That's why I was doing this. Every step, every touch, and every kiss on this walk was calculated to rile him up, to push him toward making a move. I needed him to strike. The sooner he did, the sooner this nightmare could end, and Tildie and I could finally move forward with our lives.

We reached a small clearing, and I stopped, pulling her close. She looked up at me, a question in her eyes. Before she could ask, I leaned down and kissed her.

Her lips were soft, warm, and hesitant at first, but she relaxed into the kiss, her hands resting on my chest. I let myself get lost in the moment, in her. This wasn't just for show; it was a promise—a reminder of what I was fighting for.

Then, in the distance, I heard it.

The sharp rustle of branches and the sudden flurry of birds taking flight from the trees. The sound was faint, but it was enough.

He was out there, watching.

And he was furious.

My pulse quickened, but I kept my expression calm, not wanting to alarm Tildie. My arm around her tightened protectively as I scanned the tree line. I couldn't see him, but I could feel his rage—palpable and suffocating, like a storm waiting to break.

This was it. I'd poked the beast, and now he wanted blood.

I kissed Tildie again, longer this time, letting my lips linger on hers as if to drive the point home. Mouth was out there, and he was boiling with anger. Good. I wanted him to be reckless. I wanted him to strike at me, not her.

"Let's head back," I said softly, signing the words for her. She nodded, oblivious to the danger lurking just beyond the trees.

As we walked back toward the clubhouse, I kept her close, my hand firm on her lower back. My thoughts raced, running through the plan over and over. I only prayed that my assumptions were correct —that he wouldn't kill me immediately.

If I was wrong, I was screwed.

But for Tildie, for her safety and her future, it was a risk I was willing to take.

18

I got to work without incident, but I couldn't shake the jittery feeling that came with being a walking target. It felt strange to be back at The Unlimited after months away, and already, I missed Tildie.

"Long time no see," Mandy called from her usual spot at the bar.

Mandy, Soldier's wife, was a familiar face around here. She often stopped by after work to have dinner with him. She was a great woman, and I couldn't help but feel bad for her. Soldier was carrying the weight of his issues in silence, and if he didn't open up to her soon, he'd lose her—and that would destroy him. But secrets don't stay buried forever.

"Yeah, it's been a while," I replied. "Tildie's finally well enough to be on her own."

"That's great! The last time I saw her, she was still in a leg cast. Tildie is such a sweet person. I hate that she had to go through all that."

"Me too," I admitted. "But she's healing and getting stronger every day."

Soldier appeared, grinning as he wrapped an arm around Mandy's waist. "Let's go, Dove. It's your favorite tonight—pizza," he said, kissing her nose playfully. Then he glanced at me. "Be back in an hour, Reader."

"Got it. I'll watch the floor. Later, man," I replied, watching them leave.

Taking up a position near the dance floor, I scanned the room. Most nights were uneventful, but with alcohol involved, you never knew when things might turn south.

I couldn't help wondering what Tildie was up to. It was after seven, so she was probably reading. I sent her a quick text to check in, and she replied, confirming she was curled up in her bedroom with a book. Her messages always made me smile. Even from afar, she had a way of bringing me peace.

Last night replayed in my mind. It had been incredible. Waking up with her in my arms after finally breaking through the walls she'd built was a feeling I couldn't put into words. I knew how much trust it had taken for her to let me in, and I would never betray that trust.

The hours dragged on, each tick of the clock slower than the last. While keeping an eye on the floor, a dark-haired woman approached me. She looked to be in her twenties, dressed in a skirt so short and a top so skimpy it left nothing to the imagination.

"Hey, gorgeous," she purred, her brown eyes sharp and calculating. "You look lonely standing here by yourself. I'm Alicia, and I make damn good company."

I was used to women hitting on me while working here, but there was something off about her. Her eyes gave her away—too focused, too intent. Then I noticed the phone in her hand, its screen faintly glowing. It was recording.

This was a setup.

It didn't take a genius to figure out she was working for Mouth, trying to bait me into something that could ruin what I had with Tildie. That bastard had no idea who he was dealing with. Nothing and no one would ever tempt me to betray her.

Without a word, I turned and walked away, leaving Alicia standing there. I wasn't playing Mouth's game.

But her presence meant Mouth was close, and tonight could be the night he made his move.

I was ready. Nervous, sure, but ready. Tildie was worth the pain I knew was coming.

As the clock neared midnight, Silver walked into the club. His unexpected appearance threw me off. Silver rarely came here, especially not this late.

"What are you doing here? I thought your old man ass would be in bed," I teased when he reached me.

"This old ass found out what you're trying to do," he said, his expression serious. "And I'm not letting you go in alone. If they take you, they're taking me too."

"I'll be fine, Silver. There's no guarantee they'll even take you," I argued.

"Oh, they'll take me," he shot back. "I'll be hanging off you like a whore on a millionaire." His face was set, his tone final.

"I can't ask you to put yourself in danger," I said, trying again.

"Who says you asked? I do what I fucking please, and I'm not letting you go in alone. That's final. I already told Shadow, so he knows what to expect. You're like a son to me, and I'll have your back."

I sighed, realizing there was no talking him out of it. "I suppose I don't have a choice, do I?"

"Nope," he replied. "Now let's head to your bike. I saw some shady characters at the end of the lot. My guess is they're here for you. I'll act drunk, so it looks like you're helping me. Viking's on the security monitors. This better be worth it, and we better get Cross and Mouth."

As we stepped into the parking lot, Silver draped an arm over my shoulders, playing the role of a drunk to perfection.

We didn't make it far before the men struck. Guns pressed to our heads, and rough hands grabbed us, shoving us toward a blue van.

Normally, we could've fought our way out, but this time, we let them lead us. They needed to think they'd won.

Inside the van, I stayed calm, my heart steady. I trusted my brothers. They were already in motion.

This would be over soon. For Tildie, it had to be.

19

The men shoved us down, tying our hands and feet as the van sped off. Once we were bound, they leaned us against the van's wall. There were only three of them in the vehicle, and from the lack of beatings, I knew none of them were Mouth. They kept their focus on us but didn't speak, their silence unnerving.

After what felt like an eternity—though it was only about an hour—the van jerked to a stop. The door was thrown open, and a huge, bald man stood silhouetted in the frame. His angry eyes locked onto mine, his lips curled into a snarl.

This was Mouth.

The sight of him sent my blood boiling. My anger burned hotter as I thought of everything Tildie had endured at his hands. His sheer size compared to her petite frame made it clear how terrified she must have been.

Mouth wasted no time dragging me out of the van, throwing me on the ground. He stood above me as he snarled, "I'm going to kill you nice and slow right in front of Tildie once I have her back. You touched what belongs to me and will pay. Matilda is mine and always has been, you stupid young fuck." He followed his word with a sharp kick to my ribs, the pain causing me to inhale sharply. "Take both these fuckers to the basement and string them up," Mouth growled to the men.

They dragged us into a building. It was a bar, dark and reeking of an odor I couldn't begin to describe. About twenty club members and a few women lounged around, laughing, drinking, and having sex. I scanned the room, my gaze landing on a man buttoning his jeans and heading toward us. His smirk grew as he got closer.

Cross.

"Well, well, what do we have here? Devil's House trash?" Cross sneered, his voice oozing with mockery. His eyes narrowed as he recognized Silver. "Silver, it's been a long time. Four years, isn't it? Wasn't expecting to see you, but hey, a welcome surprise. I owe you some payback for your part in killing my old man."

Without warning, he punched Silver hard in the face. Silver didn't flinch; he just smiled, blood staining his teeth.

Cross turned to the others. "Get them to the basement. Let's see if he's still smiling when we're done."

The men hauled us into the basement, where our hands were tied to the ceiling. Only our toes touched the floor, our bodies stretched painfully. I already knew I'd be hurting in minutes, but I gritted my teeth, determined to endure it.

Mouth and Cross entered, Cross holding up his phone to snap pictures. He smirked as he sent them to Shadow, clearly expecting some sort of trade. Once he was satisfied, Mouth stepped forward, his gaze dark and dangerous.

"I'm going to hurt you so fucking bad for touching Tildie," he growled, driving a fist into my gut. Blow after blow landed—my face, my ribs, my chest—until I was coughing up blood and gasping for air.

I glanced at Silver. His face was calm, his body seemingly unaffected, but his eyes burned with quiet rage.

"Easy, Mouth," Cross warned. "Don't kill him yet. Not until I have Shadow—and you have Tildie."

He was a fool if he thought Shadow would trade himself or Tildie.

Mouth leaned closer, his face twisted with fury. "You brainwashed my little girl, turned her against me so you could have her for yourself." He backhanded me hard, the metallic taste of blood flooding my mouth.

"You're one big perverted fuck," I rasped through swollen lips. "Preying on a young girl and raping her."

The punch that followed hit my temple, and darkness swallowed me whole.

I woke to the sound of Silver's voice, faint and urgent. "Reader, wake up."

Groaning, I forced my eyes open, the pain in my head pounding like a drum. Everything swam in and out of focus, but I managed to lock onto Silver's face.

"Our help has arrived," he whispered. "Shit's going down."

Then I heard it—the sound of gunfire upstairs. Women screamed, footsteps pounded, and voices shouted orders.

"Fuck!" Silver hissed as Cross's voice cut through the chaos.

"How the fuck did they find us?" Cross barked, his words fading as he and several others slipped through a hidden door in the basement wall.

More men rushed through the room, some fleeing out the hidden exit. Mouth was among them, but instead of escaping, he turned, a gun in his hand.

"I won't let you have my sweet Matilda," he roared, aiming at my chest.

The crack of the gunshot was deafening, but Silver reacted instantly, kicking Mouth's arm. The shot veered off course, hitting my shoulder in a fiery blaze of pain.

Before Mouth could recover, another shot rang out, and he crumpled to the floor.

Vampire, Shadow, and Viking stormed into the basement, their weapons drawn, their faces grim. I tried to focus as they worked to cut me down, my vision swimming as Viking pressed a hand to my bleeding shoulder.

"You're fucking lucky, Reader," he muttered, his voice steady but sharp. "It looks like the bullet missed anything vital, but Doc will have to check you over."

I wanted to reply, to say something smart, but the pounding in my head and the pain in my body were too much. Darkness beckoned again, but as I slipped under, one thought stayed clear:

Mouth was dead, and Tildie was safe.

Something was wrong. Travis didn't come home last night. I waited as long as I could, even sending him a message, but I got no response. Worry settled in my chest like a heavy weight. It was now six in the morning, and I hadn't slept a wink. The tension clawed at me, so I decided to get dressed and head to the kitchen, knowing Jane would already be up starting breakfast.

As I stepped into the hallway, I collided with a hard body. The impact sent me reeling, and I stumbled back, nearly falling, but a pair of strong hands caught me before I could hit the ground. Looking up, I saw Viking, his tall frame towering over me.

Out of the corner of my eye, I caught movement—someone being carried in on a stretcher. My heart froze. I knew it was Travis. Mouth had hurt him, and it was all because of me.

I tried to push past Viking, desperate to see Travis, but he held me firmly, his hands gripping my arms as he lowered himself to eye level. His expression was calm, but his tone was serious. "Reader will be okay," he assured me. "He's just a little banged up. Doc will take care of him, and when he's ready, I'll come get you. Nikki is here, and she'll sit with you, okay?"

I searched his face, looking for cracks in his words, but his calm demeanor didn't ease my panic. Travis was on a stretcher—he couldn't walk. How could that be "okay"?

Before I could argue, Viking stepped back, and Nikki appeared at my side, her hand gently taking mine. She was trying to guide me away from the infirmary, but I dug my heels in and refused to move. My frustration boiled over, and I pulled out my notebook, furiously scribbling:

Dammit, I am not a child! I deserve to know what's going on!

Nikki's eyes widened in surprise. She wasn't used to seeing me this way, and I didn't care. I was done being kept in the dark. Travis was hurt, and I had a right to know what had happened.

After a moment, Nikki sighed, running a hand through her long blond hair. "You're right," she said softly. "You're not a child, and I'm sorry. Come with me to the kitchen, and I'll tell you what I know. It's not much, but you deserve the truth."

I followed her to the kitchen, my heart pounding. Inside, Jane was tending to Silver, who looked like he'd been in a fight. Cuts and bruises covered his face, and one eye was swollen shut. My chest tightened— he must have been with Travis.

Without hesitation, I marched over to him and scribbled furiously:

Were you with Travis? I'm worried about him.

Silver stared at the note, his good eye scanning the words. For a moment, I thought he wouldn't answer, but then he sighed and said, "The boy's fine. Took a beating and a shot to the shoulder, but it's nothing a little care and rest won't fix. Doc just needs to patch him up. Trust me—when Reader wakes up, you'll be the first person he asks for. So don't worry. He wouldn't want that."

Relief washed over me, and I felt tears prick my eyes. Travis was okay. Battered and hurt, but okay. Silver's words were firm, and I trusted him.

I quickly wrote: **Thank you so much, Silver.**

"No thanks needed," he replied gruffly. "Now grab some breakfast and relax until Doc is done with him." He waved me off, letting Jane continue her work.

I sat down beside Nikki, letting her take my hand in hers. She rubbed small circles on my palm, trying to soothe me, but it was impossible to relax. My mind was spinning. Travis was hurt because of me, and the thought of losing him was unbearable.

I love him so much.

How was I supposed to sit here and wait, knowing he was in pain? This was going to be the longest morning of my life.

20

The murmur of voices stirred me from unconsciousness. I groaned as a sharp, searing pain spread through my body with even the slightest movement. What the hell was wrong with me?

"Reader, can you hear me?" Doc's familiar voice cut through the haze, firm and commanding. Why was Doc here?

I kept my eyes shut, willing myself to piece together the fragments of my memory. Then it hit me like a punch to the gut—Mouth had fucking shot me. Panic surged through me. *Where is Tildie?* My eyes flew open, and I tried to sit up, but the effort sent a wave of fiery pain rippling through me. I collapsed back onto the bed, a groan of anguish escaping my throat.

"Don't do that, Reader." Doc's stern voice was laced with frustration. "You need to stay still. Let me check your stitches to make sure you didn't pull them open with that dumb move." He leaned over me, his practiced hands gentle but firm.

My eyes scanned the room frantically until they landed on her — Tildie. She was sitting by my bedside, her beautiful face filled with worry. Relief washed over me. She was safe. I stretched my hand toward her, and she immediately took it, her grip warm and reassuring. Her lips curved into a small smile, though her eyes glistened with unshed tears.

Doc straightened after inspecting me, his expression softening. "Your stitches are still intact. But listen to me—you need to stay in bed and rest for a few weeks. You're weak from the gunshot wound and the beating. I got the bullet out, so your shoulder will heal just fine. You're lucky it missed a major artery."

He shifted his gaze to Tildie, who had been watching him intently, reading his lips. "I've given Tildie instructions for your care since she's agreed to nurse you back to health," he added with a wink in her direction.

Tildie blushed, and I couldn't help but tease, despite the ache in my body. "What a turn of events," I said with a smirk. "Here I am, bedridden and being taken care of by a beautiful nurse. I just hope she takes advantage of me."

Her cheeks turned an even deeper shade of pink as her eyes darted away, especially since Doc was still in the room. He chuckled, shaking his head. "I'll leave you two alone. Try to behave, Reader." With that, he left, closing the door softly behind him.

As soon as we were alone, I reached for Tildie, pulling her closer. "Don't worry, Tildie. I'll be okay. The important thing is that Mouth is gone. He can't hurt you anymore."

Tildie's lips quivered, and she pulled her hand from mine to sign, "I was so worried, so sick with fear that something had happened to you. I love you so much." Her tears fell freely now, streaking her cheeks.

I cupped her face gently, brushing away the tears with my thumb.

"I love you too, Tildie. Nothing will take me away from you. I'm sorry I worried you, but there was no other way. And I'm not sorry—I'd do it all again if it meant freeing you from that bastard." I pulled her into my arms, holding her as close as my battered body would allow.

She pulled back just enough to look at me, her expression shifting to one of fierce determination. "Don't you ever do this to me again, Travis Baylor. My heart can't take it." Her hands moved sharply, emphasizing every word.

I chuckled softly, despite the pain it caused. "I promise, Tildie. No more reckless plans." Then, unable to resist, I added with a sly grin, "Now, do I get any special privileges from my nurse? Some special medicine to make me feel better?"

Her lips twitched, and she gave me the smile I loved so much—the one that lit up her entire face. "That depends on how good the patient is," she signed, her playful expression softening the tension in the room.

"That's a challenge I'll happily take on," I replied, my voice full of affection.

As she settled back into her chair, still holding my hand, I silently vowed to spend the rest of my life ensuring that smile never left her face. She was my everything, and for her, I'd endure any pain, take any risk, and fight any battle.

21

Tildie

Epilogue

One month has passed since Travis was shot. He's fully healed and back to work, though I'd be lying if I said I didn't miss having him at home. While he was bedridden, I fussed over him relentlessly, worried I might be overbearing, but Travis assured me he loved every minute of it. Secretly, I cherished that time too. It felt good to care for him the way he had always cared for me. And, yes, he did receive a few special favors from his personal nurse.

Since then, life has been a whirlwind. Doc found several hearing specialists for me, and I've undergone so many tests that it's been exhausting. The results were a mix of good and bad news. The bad news: I am completely deaf, and it's irreversible. Nothing can change that. But the good news is that my vocal cords are perfectly fine, which means I can learn to talk with the right guidance.

That's where Grace comes in—Stonewall's older sister. She recently moved back to the area and specializes in working with deaf patients. She's agreed to take me on as a speech therapy patient. Grace also works with survivors of abuse, which Travis thinks will help me process everything that happened with Mouth. I'm not sure yet if I'm ready for that, but I'll decide after I meet her.

Today, though, all of that feels a world away. Travis has planned a special outing for us, and we've ridden his bike up to a secluded lake in the mountains. The sun is warm, and the light shimmers off the water like a thousand tiny diamonds. We're sitting on a blanket by the lakeshore, the quiet sounds of nature surrounding us. For the first time in forever, I feel completely at peace.

As I lean back against a tree, watching the ripples in the water, Travis shifts beside me. He lays a brightly wrapped package on my lap, and the shiny yellow paper catches my eye. I look at him, surprised. "What is this?" I asked, my hands hovering over the gift.

"It's a gift for you. Open it," he said, smiling, though I notice the faintest hint of nerves in his expression.

Carefully, I begin unwrapping the box, making sure not to tear the beautiful paper. I lay it neatly aside and lift the lid. Inside is a stunning special edition of *Pride and Prejudice*. The leather cover is embossed with gold details, and the craftsmanship is exquisite. My breath catches as I run my fingers over the cover.

"Travis, it's beautiful," I signed, overwhelmed. "Thank you. I love it."

"There's more," he said, smiling softly, nodding toward the book. "Read the inscription inside."

Curious, I open the book, and my heart stops. Written in Travis's familiar handwriting is a message that makes my vision blur with tears.

To Tildie,

The only woman I will ever love. You are my Elizabeth Bennet, and I want nothing more than to be your Mr. Darcy. Will you marry me?

Yours forever, Travis

I look up, my lips trembling with emotion, and see Travis kneeling in front of me. In one hand, he's holding a delicate ring that sparkles in the sunlight, and in the other, a property cut with my name embroidered on it. His warm brown eyes are filled with love and a touch of vulnerability.

"Will you, Tildie?" he asked, his eyes searching mine. "Will you be my wife and ol' lady?"

Tears spill down my cheeks as I nod fervently, my hands shaking as I signed, *"Yes. Yes!"* I throw my arms around him with such force that we both tumble onto the blanket, laughing.

Travis rolls us over, pinning me beneath him, his grin infectious. "You just made me the happiest man alive," he said before leaning down and kissing me deeply. The world fades away as I lose myself in the feel of his lips, his love radiating from every touch.

When we finally pull apart, I can't stop smiling. I trace the lines of his face, memorizing every detail. "I never thought I'd have this," I signed, my face filled with emotion. "You've given me everything I've ever dreamed of."

"And I'll keep giving you more," Travis promised, his face full of conviction. "You're my world, Tildie. Now and forever."

As we lay there by the lake, the future stretches out before us, bright and full of promise. For the first time in my life, I believe in happy endings.

Dreams do come true.

The End

* * *

The first book in the South Carolina Series: Bolt's Flame. Available Now.

* * *

* * *

About The Author

Mhairi O'Reilly

Mhairi O'Reilly lives in Upstate, South Carolina. A native of West Virginia, Mhairi loves to read, Devoting many hours of her life to it. She always dreamed of writing her own stories; when the time arrived that she had the time, she jumped into it, not looking back.

Made in the USA
Columbia, SC
04 March 2025

54673210R00067